Good Girls Always Got a Thing for the Thugs

K.L. Hall

B. Love Publications

Synopsis

Clover

I'm the definition of a good girl—the kind that lives in my scrubs and crocs and helps save lives.

As an emergency department nurse, I'm practically married to my career, which helps, being that my heart's been on ice since the death of my fiancé two years ago. So no, I'm not interested in love or revisiting that type of pain—not until I meet a foul-mouthed bad boy whose smile makes my yoni weep.

Harlan Banks is the president of The Spades, a ruthless MC club in the Chi. My attraction to him was instant, one of the most intense connections I've ever experienced. When his lips touch mine, they jumpstart my soul and make me want to expose all my scars. Being in his warm arms may be the key to thawing my icy heart.

Harlan

Being a member of The Spades took me from a boy to a savage. Now, as the leader, I live and die by the code of my brotherhood: to stay loyal and never give up the fight. My life's mission is to find whoever killed my brother and put them in a body bag. Nothing is more important than my revenge—until her.

Known on the streets as "Harlan the Heartless", I've witnessed the worst parts of life.

But ever since my chaos collided with her calm, I crave to experience all the good life has to offer with her by my side.

Everything changes when I learn a war is brewing with a rival gang, making it the worst time for my heart to get in the way. But when her past catches up with us, her survival becomes my only priority.

Death doesn't scare me. Losing *her* does.

CLOVER BALDWIN

I t was two o'clock in the morning, and I was nearing my eighteenth hour on my feet in the emergency department. I was so exhausted I practically saw double as I sat at the nurse's station doing paperwork. My friend and fellow ED nurse, Quintessa, came over to me with a frustrated look on her face. I made an X with my arms, crossing them in front of my face before she could even part her lips to speak.

"Whatever it is, the answer is no," I told her.

"Girl, you won't believe this shit!" she huffed.

Q rarely cursed on the floor, so I knew it had to be serious. I slowly lowered my arms and gave her my full attention. "Wassup?"

She rolled her brown eyes while folding her arms across her busty chest. "Why is my fuckin' sister in bay seven with her mayonnaise-colored boyfriend?"

My brows shot up. "Her what? Why?"

"I don't know. I saw her being rolled in on a gurney, wearing a trench coat and Timberlands with no socks, and I marched my ass right over here. I've been working for sixteen hours straight. I'm *not* dealing with this shit! She's family, so I can't treat her bigheaded ass anyway."

Jesus, be a fence. "What you want me to do, Q?" I asked, knowing she was about to ask for a favor.

"Go see why she's here, and only report back if it's something life-threatening. I'm talkin' like that bitch needs a kidney transplant, not like appendicitis or some shit."

I rolled my eyes. "Can't you get somebody else to do it? I've been on my feet since eight o'clock yesterday morning," I whined.

"Please. If it were anybody else, I wouldn't even ask, but you know I can only deal with her for so long when I'm sober."

I couldn't help but chuckle. "Fine, but you owe me a chai tea latte, a big one, too!"

"Yeah, yeah, add it to my tab."

My legs propelled me over to bay seven, and I pulled the curtain back to see Quintessa's younger sister, Quiana, lying on the bed with a frazzled look on her face.

"Hey there, Quiana. What brings you in?" I queried while pulling up her chart.

"Is Quintessa here? Lachlan thought he saw her when we came in," she replied, referring to her boyfriend.

"She's running around here somewhere. The ED has been a bit of a madhouse all night."

"Okay, well, can you tell her that her baby sister is here?"

"Sure will. But let's talk about what's going on with you. It says here on your intake form that you're having some pain in your vaginal cavity?"

The emergency room was one of the last places anyone wanted to be, so I kept my composure. Plus, she was my girl's sister, and I wanted her to feel comfortable so I could ensure she was properly treated.

Her pasty boyfriend immediately clammed up from embarrassment. "I'll be outside," he muttered before disappearing behind the curtain.

Quiana cleared her throat before parting her lips to explain. "Well, Lachlan and I had gotten tipsy and decided to get a lil freaky. He suggested we spice things up and said he had a surprise for me in the bedroom. When we got back there, he pulled out a vibrating... cock ring."

I brought my hand to my mouth to stifle my laughter as she continued. "Instead of using it the 'normal way,' we decided to take things to the next level and put it inside me. At first, it was cool. The sex was wet and wild. This may be T.M.I., but my orgasms were *super* intense. But the freakier things got, the deeper it went."

"Holy shit," I mumbled under my breath.

"I didn't wanna come to the ER because of Quinny and how *embarrassing* this is. So, at first, he did some fishing around in there but didn't feel anything. My God, I never thought I'd see the day when I *wanted* to stop cumming. Thank God we got the vibrating to stop, but we still can't get it to come out," she confessed.

I'd been working in the ED at Lakeside Memorial Hospital for almost four years and had seen my share of sexual misadventures but nothing as funny as hers.

"Okay, girl. Don't worry, we're going to have the doctor come take a look and see if we can get that cock ring right out," I reassured her, realizing how crazy it sounded the minute the words slipped past my lips.

"Thanks, girl."

"No problem."

A couple of muscle relaxants and a pair of medical pliers later, the cock ring was out. It was the raunchy equivalent of a child getting a penny or a bead jammed up their nose. After promising me she wouldn't laugh or make a scene, Quintessa joined me in handing her sister her discharge papers.

"The doctor signed off on your discharge papers, so you can get dressed and head out," I announced.

Quintessa spoke up. "How are you feeling?"

"Much better now."

"Good, because you know I'm never, *ever, ever, ever* letting your ass live this down, right?" she asked her sister, chuckling.

Quiana rolled her eyes. "Shut up! I'm embarrassed enough as it is!"

"Tuh! As you should be."

Before I could join in on their banter, Quiana's phone dinged. She looked at the screen before quickly locking it so that it went black. "Shit."

"What?"

Quiana huffed. "Lachlan wants to know what happened to the... *ring* and if we can, uh, get it back?"

Quintessa made a retching sound as if she were vomiting, and I screwed up my face as well. "Uh, I think it's gone in the medical waste," I informed her.

"Where it belongs!" Quintessa added with a disgusted look on her chestnut-brown face.

"That's fine. I've had my fill of that shit anyway, no pun intended."

"This is what you get for fuckin' on that Ken doll of yours. Wouldn't no Black dick have you in the ED in the middle of the night lookin' crazy with some wild shit all in your hot pocket!"

"Why are you so mad that I learned how to game the system before you?"

Q rolled her eyes. "Here we go again."

"I'm just sayin'. I get my back blown or my na-na tongued down in the nastiest way possible, and I never ever put a pink dick in my mouth. Either way, I figure it's the closest thing to reparations I'll ever get."

"It's the ignorance for me," Quintessa huffed while shaking her head in a swift arc.

"Y'all can keep fuckin' on the chocolate broke ones all you want. That's just more white meat for me."

"Keep it. I'll take the big, black dick for two hundred, Alex."

Q and I shared a laugh while her sister redressed. "Laugh all y'all want, but I don't fuck with niggas because they never knew how to act, *ever*. Games are for kids, and baby, I'm grown, grown," Quiana boasted.

"Obviously not grown enough to use a cock ring properly." Her sister snickered.

Quiana turned to me. "Clover, what's your one ho goal for the year?" she asked out of the blue.

My forehead creased. "I'm sorry, my what?"

"You heard me correctly—"

Quintessa interjected. "Please excuse my delusional ass baby sister. Just because she's hard-pressed on fucking every white devil out there don't mean we all gotta be gettin' colonized with her ass."

I chuckled. "That damn Jack Harlow got all the white boys feelin' themselves these days, huh?"

"Y'all say whatever y'all want, but ever since a nigga with a big, black dick broke my heart, I *only* allow white men to service my needs."

"Oh my God, Qui. I promise you nobody cares!" Quintessa argued. "And speaking of white men, where is your vanilla flavor of the week?"

Quiana looked over her shoulders before spilling the tea. "He's around. Shit, even if I got a man, I *still* got a ho goal."

"I'm too curious not to ask what that is," I admitted.

Quiana shrugged her twenty-one-year-old shoulders. "C'mon, what would you do if you could only be a ho for a lil bit? Whose dick would you sit on? You're in charge of the pussy, so you make the rules!"

Amusement pinwheeled across my face. "I can't say I have a ho goal, and I'm gonna skip making one."

Sex had been the last thing on my mind since the death of my fiancé, Lorenzo, two years prior. I hadn't had or wanted any human interaction down there since. I didn't date in person or through apps. I wasn't hip to the latest music and didn't frequent the clubs. After losing Leo, working at the hospital and helping to save lives became my life's purpose. So no, I wasn't riding the faces of Ken dolls every night like Quiana, nor was I in the market for a nigga with a big, black dick like Q. But what they didn't know wouldn't hurt me.

"And you know I don't play that dumb shit," Quintessa chimed in.

"Both of y'all's old asses should come out with me."

"Mmmm, hard pass!" Q spat, waving off her sister. They were six years apart but acted like they'd grown up in different generations. "I need high levels of melanin in my places of litness, not whatever season-less shit you on."

"Fine. We'll go somewhere you want."

"When?"

"This weekend. Better yet, this Friday."

"Y'all have fun. I think I'm gonna sit this one out."

"Why? If I gotta go, so do you!" Quintessa declared.

"Because I-I have plans," I stammered.

Q shook her head. "I know you're off this Friday, so you can't use work as an excuse."

I huffed, giving up quickly because I couldn't think of a better lie. "Shit. Okay, you got me."

"C'mon, girl. When do you *ever* leave this place? You pick up extra shifts on holidays and weekends. It's like you're purposely trying not to have a life."

"Shut up! It's not like that," I argued.

"Yeah, okay."

I smacked my lips. "Whatever. Fine, I'll go."

Her brows lifted in surprise at my change of heart. "For real?"

"Mmhm."

Q rolled her eyes toward the ceiling. "This bitch bluffin'."

"No, I'm not. I'm serious. I'll go to whatever spot y'all pick on Friday; just text me the address."

"Mmm, so your ass can dip out early or show up late? No, ma'am. If we do this, we do it right. I'm picking you up myself," Q asserted.

"There's no way I'm getting out of this, is there?" I challenged.

"Nope," they answered in unison.

———

Friday rolled around quicker than I'd anticipated. Between working crazy hours and doing next to nothing in my downtime, I never went to the mall to buy something to wear. I snapped my knees straight while standing in my closet, surveying my bland options. My arms laced over my chest just as my phone rang.

"Hello?" I answered as I sifted through my closet hangers.

"I'm getting Quiana now, and then I'ma pull up on you in about fifteen. You almost ready?"

I huffed. "No. I hate everything in my closet. All I have are scrubs and like, two skirts."

"Damn, it's worse than I thought. You need me to tell my sister to grab you somethin' hoochie-fied to wear before she come out my mama house?" Quintessa inquired.

My forehead bunched. "Ugh. I think I might."

"Okay, say less. Let me call her. We'll see you soon."

I ended the call, and my chest deflated with a sigh. If I were going to get through the night, I would need some liquid courage. Since Quintessa agreed to be the designated driver, I decided to start the party early.

I charged into the kitchen and grabbed the bottle of tequila from the back of the freezer. After tossing back a few swigs and screwing up my face, I finally started to feel warm all over. *Relax, Clo. It's just one night. A change of scenery and attire couldn't hurt.*

I was raised in one of the most affluent Chicago suburbs. Growing up, my only sibling was our cocker spaniel, Rosie. Aside from her, I only had a handful of friends from my private school days, most of whom I lost touch with after graduation. Because Quintessa and I spent so much time together at the hospital, it was only natural we clicked and became friends outside of work.

When Quintessa arrived, she tossed me three outfit options and sent me to my room to change. I came out ten minutes later wearing the second outfit. It was a sequined, one-shoulder, black mini dress with gold flames, a small side slit, and the least revealing of the three.

"You look good, girl," Quinn commented from the kitchen.

She wore a bronze metallic dress that stopped above her chocolate knees, and her long box braids were swept up into a high bun on the crown of her head.

"Thanks. I'm just glad it fits. Y'all ready to go?"

"Yup!" Quiana answered, pulling herself up from the couch. She was clad in a rhinestone romper with long sleeves, an open back, and lace-up details that accentuated her DD breasts and thick thighs.

"All right, ladies, let's go turn up!" Quintessa cheered as we headed toward the door.

"So, where exactly are we going?" I probed once I folded my body into the passenger seat of Quintessa's SUV.

"Onyx," Quiana answered.

"What's that?"

"A poppin' bar on the outskirts of the city."

"A bar?"

"Yeah. On Fridays, they have trivia nights. I figured you'd like it," Quintessa added.

"Trivia night, eh?" I quizzed, smelling a lie.

Quiana snickered in the back seat, which made me even more suspicious. "Here, drink up," she encouraged, passing me an airplane bottle of tequila.

The rest of the ride consisted of liquor and lip-synching the latest hip-hop and R&B hits. When we pulled into the parking lot inside the large shopping center, Quintessa killed the engine and tossed back a shot before getting out. I smelled the gasoline and burnt rubber in the air the minute I exited Q's vehicle. My eyes scanned the sprawling parking lot before spotting the bar bathed in neon lights at the edge of the shopping center. There were dozens, if not hundreds, of motorcycles and sports cars all lined up, some revving their turbocharged engines as we walked by. I tugged at the hem of my dress, immediately feeling overdressed for the occasion. The large lot was crawling with niggas of all colors and creeds bumping their music loud.

"Damn. All the ballers are out tonight showing off their dope ass rides," Quiana marveled.

"Bag back, lil sis. I thought you only liked your meat undercooked."

I cut my eyes at Quintessa. "I thought you said tonight was trivia night."

"Did I?" she inquired, tilting her head to the side.

"Yes! All I see are fast cars and vintage motorcycles!"

She shrugged. "Oops. Guess it's a car meet or something going on out here."

"Or *something*?"

"Relax! I'm about to get us some drinks as soon as we get inside. The first round is on me!" Quintessa announced as she pushed open the door to the bar.

The smoky air inside the dimly lit bar hummed with the low growl of conversation and the clinking of tequila-filled shot glasses. I immediately started coughing from the harsh stench of marijuana and cigarettes permeating the air. There was a small DJ booth near the main stage where men clad in leather jackets and worn boots were watching a wet T-shirt contest.

I grabbed Q's arm, partially for safety and partially for stability so I didn't bust my ass in my four-inch heels. "Girl, what the hell is going on in here? I'm feeling *extremely* overstimulated."

"All those shots you had on the way here, and your ass is still *this* uptight? C'mon, I'll make sure the bartender makes you a double!"

She hooked her arm in mine and led us over to the bar, where we threw back our first round of shots. After dancing to a couple of songs at our table, I could finally feel myself loosening up.

"Y'all ready for the next round? I'm buyin'," I offered.

"Well, in that case," Quiana replied with a chuckle, "I'm ready!"

"I'm down, too."

"Cool. Three shots of tequila coming right up. I'll be back!" I hollered over the music.

Lil Wayne was on his second verse of "Lollipop" when the DJ mixed in "Go DJ". The bass was so powerful I could've sworn I felt the floor rattling underneath me. I approached the bar and waved down the bartender. It wasn't hard to see she was swamped, so I didn't mind the wait. My eyes surveyed the space around me before zeroing in on a man standing at the opposite end of the bar. His soft, airbrushed cinnamon-brown skin was covered in black ink. Diamond studs sparkled in his ears, complementing the gold chain around his neck and the leather jacket on his back. His haircut and well-groomed facial hair were fresh to death. I wanted to get closer so I could see more. I was *that* invested. I took one step forward, and my breath hitched as soon as his eyes locked with mine. It was like a moment suspended in time. We maintained a flawless connection for a few seconds until I nervously tore my eyes away. In an instant, all my courage dissolved. The bartender approached me.

"What can I get you?" she requested, pulling my attention away from him.

"Oh, uh, three shots of tequila, please."

"Light or dark?"

"Light."

"You startin' a tab, or you want to pay now?"

"I'll pay now," I answered before digging inside my clutch for my card.

Once I handed it over, I looked back to where I'd seen the fine-ass mystery man, who was now gone. I did a visual sweep of the bar, and it was as if he'd disappeared into thin air.

"Here you go," the bartender said, returning my card before lining up three shot glasses and pouring tequila to the rim.

"Thanks," I mumbled, gaze still hunting him as I tossed my shot back.

With the two drinks in my hands, I returned to Q and her sister. "Girl, I just saw the finest nigga at the bar," I blabbed while passing them their shots.

"Oh yeah. Where'd he go?"

I shrugged. "That's the thing. I don't know," I admitted, casting my eyes around the bar for the thousandth time.

"Did you talk to him?" Quiana queried.

"No. I didn't get a chance to. All we did was trade glances, and then he disappeared. I've been looking around for him but haven't seen him since."

"Damn."

"Right. I ain't seen a nigga *that* fine in a long time," I confessed as a song by Meg Thee Stallion came on.

"Maybe he'll turn up again. In the meantime, I'm ready to be on my Coyote Ugly shit and start dancing on bar tops!" Q exclaimed while twerking.

"Hold that thought. I gotta pee, and I'm going to find the bathroom. I'll be back!" I yelled into her ear.

She nodded while swaying her body to the music, and I took off. I'd been holding my bladder for the better part of the night. I hated using public restrooms, but I couldn't hold it any longer. After locating the restrooms on the other side of the bar, I noticed the women's line was wrapped around the corner, while the men's appeared free.

"Fuck this," I mumbled before charging into the men's room.

I kept my eyes pinned to the sticky ground and headed straight for a vacant stall. After relieving my bladder and washing my hands, I pushed open the door and ran smack into the handsome stranger I'd seen earlier. "Excuse me. I-I'm sorry."

"You good, love. The fuck were you doin' in the men's bathroom?"

Looking into his rich chocolate-brown eyes had my heart all out of cadence. Feeling exposed, I linked my arms across my breasts. "Normally, I wouldn't, but the line for the ladies' room was too damn long, and the way my drunk bladder is set up, it wouldn't let me wait," I overexplained as my lashes fluttered softly.

He licked his lips before ambushing me with his dazzling white smile. My knees instantly turned to mush. "Hmm, resourceful *and* beautiful. I like that in a woman."

I nervously swept a few curls behind my ear. His hold on my mind and body was out of this world, and I didn't even know his name. I hadn't felt a connection that strong in a long time. My gaze swept from his head to his toes, cataloging his features. He had a fresh Caesar cut with tapered sides and a sea of black waves. His manicured goatee and beard, wrapped from one ear to the other, enhanced his handsome aura. I cast an exploratory look to the gold necklace with a diamond-encrusted twenty-two hanging from it and the tattoos on his neck and collarbone made visible from the V-neck shirt clinging to his fit body. Crisp jeans and boots completed his outfit.

"You ride?"

"Ride what?" I quizzed innocently.

He licked his pouty lips while laughing lightly. "Motorcycles."

I swung my head in a no. "Oh, no. I'm only here because my girls lied and told me it was trivia night."

"*Trivia*? Nah. It's a car meet. Me and a few members of my crew came out here to see what's good for the night."

"Noted."

He tilted his head to the side, allowing me to see the tattoos on his neck up close and personal. Each one told stories of loyalty and brother-hood. "So, what do you do?"

"I'm a nurse. You?"

"Really? I would have guessed you were a model or somethin'."

I cheesed. "Whatever."

"I'm the president of The Spades."

"The Spades?"

"A motorcycle club."

I nodded, noticing the club insignia on his leather jacket. The snarling viper coiled around a spade signaled he was danger and allure wrapped in one sexy ass package. "Got it." I chuckled.

"I'm Harlan," he introduced himself while extending his hand to me.

"Clover."

"That's a dope name. I saw you over at the bar earlier, right?"

I nodded. "Yeah, but hey, don't let me hold you up if you need to go."

"Go where?"

A gentle laugh tickled my throat. "The bathroom."

He cracked a smile. "Good lookin' out, *Lady Luck*."

Harlan pressed his back against the door and backed inside as his eyes snaked along my curves. His gaze spiked my adrenaline, so much so that I stood planted outside the bathroom, waiting for him as if we had unfinished business.

"Lady Luck?" I quizzed when he exited the bathroom, and his eyes landed on mine.

"Anybody ever called you that before?"

"Nope. You'd be the first," I flirted.

"Maybe I'm tryna be the only," he replied, licking his lips.

Desire dripped over my skin as I swallowed the lump in my throat. Before I had the chance to respond, he spoke up again. "So, you single?"

Although I knew the answer was simple, I still didn't feel right saying yes, especially not when I was still wearing the necklace with my engagement ring on it. "It's complicated," I answered. "You?"

"The opposite. I'm as single as a dollar bill."

"And why is that?"

His shoulders rose and fell. "Because most of these hos ain't about shit."

"Sheesh. You're a straight shooter, huh?"

He shrugged his muscular shoulders. "That's the only way I know how to be."

Just thinking about my last relationship and the past trauma made me want to switch gears or dead the conversation altogether. My fiancé, Lorenzo's, death was still a sore spot for me. He died suddenly of a brain aneurysm, and I didn't even get to say goodbye. I wasn't willing to talk about his death to the people closest to me, let alone a stranger by the bathroom in a bar, no matter how damn good he looked.

"I think I need some fresh air," I said, changing the subject.

"Let's step outside then."

Harlan slipped his hand in mine and led me outside. His chocolate brown eyes scanned the buzzing lot filled with people. A Nissan GT-R and a black and red Kawasaki revved their engines as the crowd clapped and cheered around them.

"What's going on?"

"They're about to race," Harlan informed me, still holding my hand.

"Race? Where?"

He extended his index finger to the long, straight road across from the lot. "The street."

"Is it legal?"

"Does it matter?"

I smirked before asking another question. "Do you race?"

"I used to but not much anymore."

"Why not?"

His shoulders rose and fell, but he remained silent. "So, you're a nurse, huh? Saving lives and shit?"

I nodded. "Trying my best. And you? What does the president of a motorcycle club do?"

His penetrating eyes sparkled under the city lights. "We do a lot of shit for the city like toy drives and fundraisers for kid's hospitals and homeless shelters. We ain't all savages."

"Nice."

He leaned closer. "You ever rode a motorcycle, Lady Luck?"

My pulse quickened. "Nope. Never. Bikes scare me too much."

"Stick with me, and you'll never have shit to be scared of."

I smirked. "Is that right?"

"Yeah. Plus, after you do it once and feel the wind kiss your face and the freedom pumping in your veins, you'll never wanna look back."

"You make it sound so intriguing. Who knows, maybe I'll let you take me on a ride one day."

"I'll let you ride it whenever you want."

My heart skipped a beat. "Which one is yours?" I quizzed, switching gears before our conversation went to the point of no return.

He twisted his neck to the left and pointed way across the lot. "No bike tonight. I'm in the blacked-out Hellcat over there."

"Do you know the people racing?"

"Yeah. The one on the motorcycle about to race is from my club."

"Y'all aren't scared to drive so fast?"

"The Spades don't fear death," he declared.

"I guess that gun on your waist doesn't hurt either."

He pulled his hand out of mine before slipping his arms around my waist. "You're pretty observant."

"It's a skill."

"You wanna get closer and watch the race? They're about to start."

I twisted my neck toward the bar entrance. I hadn't talked to Q or her sister since I'd gone to the bathroom. "I should probably get back inside. My girls are probably wondering where I am. That, or they're too lit to care, but I should still get back to them," I insisted.

Harlan dipped his chin. "Aight then."

A soft smile stretched across my face. "It was nice meeting you."

He pulled my hand up to his lips and kissed it. "The pleasure was all mine, Lady Luck."

I managed to escape his warm embrace without melting into a puddle of desire. Once inside, I proceeded back over to the section where I'd left Q and her sister, only to find it occupied by another group of females. "Shit. Where are they?"

I moved my eyes in a slow arc, searching for the two familiar faces I came with. I made my way toward the ladies' room and found Q standing in the doorway of one of the stalls, with Quiana retching over the toilet.

"Q? What the hell is going on?" I pressed.

"There you are! Where have you been, Clover? This dummy is drunk and throwing up. We need to hurry up and get the hell out of here," she advised.

I'd sobered up enough, so I offered to drive since Q and her sister both had ingested one too many drinks. Q passed me the keys while we worked to peel Quiana off the bathroom floor and get her to the truck. Once inside, I started the engine and put the truck in reverse. I pressed the gas and backed out of the tight space when I heard a loud crash. My foot mashed the brake while searching the rearview and side mirrors to see what I'd hit.

"Oh shit!"

"Oh my God, Clover! What the fuck did you hit?" Q yelled.

"Oh shit! Oh shit! Oh shit!" I panicked while hopping out of the truck.

I ran around the back to see Quintessa's busted taillight and a few minor scratches on the bumper. Fear splintered my bones when I turned to assess the damage to the other vehicle. Harlan was sitting behind the wheel of the black Hellcat I'd backed into. My nerves were stripped bare as embarrassment crushed my chest. I slogged over to the driver-side door and watched him get out.

"We meet again, Lady Luck."

My brows stretched toward my baby hairs. "I am soooo sorry," I pleaded, cupping my hand over my mouth. "I don't know how I didn't see you! Are you okay?"

"I'm fine. Are you okay?"

"No! I'm freaking out! This isn't even my truck. It's my friends!" I confessed.

"Chill out. Everybody is fine. That's all that matters."

I waved my head. "You're just being nice."

"Maybe I am."

My shoulders sagged defeatedly. "So much for Lady Luck, huh?"

"I still think you are."

I scoffed. "Tell that to the scratches on your bumper."

"For real. If you hadn't backed into my shit, I would've never gotten the opportunity to ask you for your number. I let you get away too easily the first time."

I stood there, trying to think of the right thing to say, but the only thing that came to me was a smile. "So, does that make me the lucky one or you?"

"Maybe we both are."

"I appreciate you trying to make me feel better."

"Only appreciate it if it's working."

"I think it is. I don't feel as nauseous as I did the minute I heard the crash," I admitted before a soft chuckle blew past my lips.

He smirked. "Good."

"Seriously, though. I have insurance! I'll give you whatever information you need. Do I give you my policy number? The license plate? I've never hit anyone before," I babbled. "Is this even drivable? Do I need to call the cops?"

He chuckled. "Relax. You're clearly too rattled to drive, although it's drivable. Why don't you let me take you home?"

"No, no. I can't ask you to do that."

"How 'bout you let me decide what I can and can't do?"

"I'm just trying to—"

"Chill. I'm fuckin' with you."

My chest deflated in relief. "You said it's drivable, right?"

"Yeah. It's just a busted taillight and some scratches. If you're going straight home, you should be straight."

"Then I have to honor the girl code."

"What's that?"

"We come together; we leave together."

"Well, in that case, let me follow you."

"No, Harlan, I can't—" I paused and huffed. "You're not going to let this go, are you?"

A quick no jerked his head. "Make friends with your ego and get over yourself, Lady Luck. I'm not takin' no for an answer."

HARLAN BANKS

Clover stepped away from me and took half of my heart with her. We hadn't spent more than twenty minutes together all night, but her bubbly vibe was infectious, and her beauty was intoxicating. The warm honey-blonde highlights in her long, wavy hair complemented her airbrushed sienna-brown complexion. Her almond-shaped, cocoa-brown eyes, button nose, and glossed lips commanded all my attention without lifting a finger. I couldn't imagine what spell I'd be under if she had really been trying to impress me. In my eyes, Clover was a radiant beauty with curves like the backroads my grandfather used to live on. Between the innocence behind her mesmerizing eyes and dazzling smile, she was the purest form of trouble. She was wrapped around my mind so tightly that no other thoughts could get through. I didn't want them to. It wasn't until we passed by the street where my brother, Harlow, was killed three months prior that my thoughts returned to the darkness I was used to.

Harlow, or Low, as I called him, was a notorious street racer with lightning-fast reflexes. For years before his death, our father owned Franklin & Sons Motors, the only Black-owned repair shop on the south side of Chicago. Consequently, Low was always in his shop with his head underneath a hood. He loved cars and engines and had an insatiable desire for the fast life—cars, bikes, and women alike. We were similar in many ways, but it was our love for cars that formed our strongest bond. Our mom used to say that as kids, whenever we couldn't sleep, she and our father would pile us all up into the car and circle the neighborhood until we drifted off. It was always the gentle roar of the engines that calmed us.

Low started working on cars at thirteen before he got interested in bikes after high school. Besides his skillful reflexes, he was good with his hands, and had a knack for business. After he graduated, he started managing the shop full-time while still running in the streets. It wasn't until I found one of his kilos buried in a stack of tires in the storage room that I made him put me on. Eventually, we took over the bills for Mama once she started having health issues and had to cut back her hours at work.

Our love for bikes, money, and camaraderie amongst our boys in the streets led us to charter The Spades. Low had been the president since its inception four years earlier, and I was his right hand. The Spades were more than a crew to me. We were a brotherhood. A merry band of drug-dealing bikers that helped turn me from a boy to a man. My boy, Chop, was our sergeant-at-arms. His government name was Cylas, but everybody called him Chop because he wasn't afraid to chop a mothafucka up when defending or protecting his brothers. Besides him, there was Nitro, our road captain, who planned all our drug runs and led us out on rides. Bricks was the secretary, keeping track of all the shipments at our trap spots around the city.

Each of our spots had steel bars on the windows, a gated entrance, and surveillance cameras throughout. We never kept any drugs at our clubhouse in case the cops showed up. Ghost was our treasurer and our accountant. He made sure we made generous monthly donations to our local homeless shelters and to the chief of police to keep the judicial system wrapped around our fingers. The club's enforcer was Taz, short for Tasmanian Devil, because his gigantic, brolic ass didn't have a problem enforcing the rules. The most important rule was no product in the clubhouse. If anybody got caught, they'd get their asses beat and then were out. Lastly, there was Doc, our tail gunner and medic. If shit ever went left, we went to him instead of the hospital unless shit was life-threatening. The rest of the members of The Spades were low-level dealers or corner boys who all loved to do two things: make money and ride fast. Aside from our clubhouse, we washed our money through our father's repair shop. Our system was flawless. We rode out of the city once a month, exchanged cash for product, and left. Any money we brought in was laundered through the shop, where we did repairs, custom work, and paint jobs.

Everything changed the night Low was killed. Suddenly, I'd gone from standing in my brother's shadow to being thrust into the spotlight. He was on his way out of town to meet with our connect when I called him because a couple of stick-up kids had hit one of our stash spots. I told him I had everything under control, but he decided to turn around and come back to the city. He was a couple of miles away when three motorcycles pulled up on him at a red light and shot up his car. He got hit thirteen times. My entire world skidded off track after I got the news. I was beyond fucked up. Everyone was on edge.

Chop wanted me to take the time I needed to rest and reset my mind, but sleeping wouldn't bring my brother back. And relaxing damn sure wouldn't bring me any closer to finding his killer. Whoever took my brother from me and The Spades deserved the fate I planned to hand-deliver. Three months was already too long to go without answers. The longer the days stretched on, the antsier I became. I was known on the streets as "Harlan the Heartless". I was going to bring down a mountain of chaos on the head of the snake that killed my brother. With the sound of a purring motorcycle behind me, I vowed to take on whoever, whenever, and never let my brothers fall.

A savage beast was raging inside me that left me always frustrated and on edge. I spent most of my nights damaging my liver with liquor and faceless bitches who didn't mean a thing to me once the sun came up. But something told me my night with Clover would be different. The control I usually maintained disappeared when she entered my chaotic world. My attraction to her was magnetic—too magnetic to not be fuckin' dangerous for the both of us.

After following her to her place as promised, I sat behind the wheel of my car and watched her hop out and hug her friends before they pulled off. She swept her hair behind her ear before flashing her eyes at my headlights and walking over. I let down the window just as she pulled up on me.

"Thanks again for, y'know, making sure I made it home okay."

I shrugged. "Not a problem, Lady Luck. What you about to get into now? You tired?" I quizzed.

She shook her head. "I should be, but I'm not. You?"

The wind blew, causing a few curls to whip across her face as the scent of coconut milk and jasmine wafted past my nose. She smelled good enough to eat.

"Nah. I'm a night owl."

"Yeah?"

"Mmhm."

"Do you wanna come up?" she blurted out, looking back at her apartment building.

I glanced at the dashboard before drawing my gaze back to her. "Sure. Let me park."

———

"I want you to know I *never* do this," Clover stated as her key jingled into her apartment's lock.

"Do what?"

"Invite people over, especially not strangers."

"Lucky me."

She smirked before glancing over her shoulder at me. "See, I told you that you were the lucky one."

I smiled back before risking a peek at her ass popping out of that dress like confetti as she stepped inside. Suddenly, a feeling I'd never experienced washed over me and erased all my calm. Instantly, I knew it was me who was in over my head, not the other way around.

"So, this is your place, huh?" I examined, glancing around at the spacious leather couch with accent pillows and hardwood floors that ran throughout.

"Yup. It's not much, but it's mine, at least for the moment."

"Got plans on flyin' away, little bird?"

She smirked. "I wanna spread these wings as far as possible."

"Where to next?"

Her shoulders rose and fell. "I'm not sure yet. I've always been one of those *go wherever the wind takes me* kinda girls. So, we'll see."

"Well, I plan to enjoy every moment of you before you fly away."

"Can I get you something to drink? I don't remember if I mentioned this earlier, but I'm an ER nurse and a workaholic, so my shifts are crazy," she chuckled.

A laugh huffed through my nostrils. "It's no problem."

"I promise you I was going somewhere with all this," she paused, baiting her breath. "Oh! Right! I work a lot, so I probably don't have shit but almond milk and water in the fridge," she admitted before walking backward toward her kitchen.

We exchanged smiles before she turned on her heels and headed to the refrigerator to verify what she did or didn't have. "Yup, just as I suspected," she said, popping out with her nose close to the open almond milk carton to give it a quick whiff. "It's old."

"Water sounds good, Lady Luck."

"It's good for you anyway, right? Plus, what better way to rehydrate our bodies after a night of drinking?"

I smirked. "Smart thinkin'."

"So, what do you do outside of your motorcycle club?"

"I run my family's repair shop."

Her perfectly arched brow. "Hold up. *You* fix cars?"

My shoulders bobbed. "Cars, bikes, anything with wheels. Tell your girl to bring her shit by. I'll give her the hook-up."

Joy flickered in her brown eyes. "Hold up. Are you for real?"

"Yup."

"Seriously, Harlan?"

I bobbed my head. "Yeah."

"Okay. Shoot me the information, and I'll let Q know. She's going to be so hype. I'm still so damn embarrassed I hit your car. I've seriously *never* done anything like that before! Completely unplanned!"

"Unplanned nights be the best ones."

She smiled. "You right."

"It got me next to you again, so a nigga ain't complainin'."

"Well, feel free to have a seat on the couch. I'm gonna go change into something more comfortable."

I arched a curious brow before nodding. "Bet."

"We need some noise in here. Throw some music on or turn on the TV," she instructed before disappearing down the hall.

I surveyed the space, looking around until I located a Bluetooth speaker on her coffee table. After pairing it with my phone, I turned on "Favorite Song" by Toosii and let it rock. Clover returned a few minutes later wearing a navy-blue crop top and a pair of gray Nike shorts. A pair of Nike crew socks adorned her feet, and her hair was swept up in a messy bun. She wore eyeglasses with green frames.

I chuckled. "Oh, so when you said comfortable, you meant just that."

"What did you think I meant?"

My shoulders rose and fell. "Nothing at all."

"You thought I was gonna come out here in a bra, panties, and some heels, huh?"

"A lil less."

She scoffed. "*Less*?"

"Just the heels," I answered.

Her brows shot up toward her baby hair. "Wow. I shouldn't be surprised since you're El Presidente and all."

I chuckled. "Yeah, well, for what it's worth, I dig the fit, and I think girls who wear glasses are sexy as fuck."

Clover cracked a smile as she joined me on the couch. "Whose song is this?"

"You haven't heard this before?"

"I can barely remember what day of the week it is most of the time. I'm not hip to any new music, and when I say new, I mean within the last year."

I dipped my chin. "Touché. Do you like it? I can change the song if you want. Let me guess, you wanna hear some Drake, right?"

Her brows crumpled. "What's wrong with Drake?"

"Nothin' wrong with that yellow ass nigga. He cool, I guess."

Clover let out a gentle puff of laughter. "Whatever, but this is a chill song. I like it. Keep it on. It's actually... pretty."

"Pretty song for a pretty girl."

We spent the next two hours talking about everything from her college major and craziest emergency room story to the first motorcycle I ever bought and bits and pieces about Low. She guessed red was my favorite color on the first try. She started smiling all wide like a kid in a candy store when I told her she was right. There was something about her innocence that made me grin. I'd never given enough of a fuck about other people's hopes and dreams, but when she talked about hers, it made me want all her desires to come true. Her soul was too beautiful not to experience happiness. Overall, we couldn't have been more different. Clover was a nurse who healed people for a living, and I was the nigga who sent mothafuckas to her. What would a tattooed bad boy like me do with a good girl like Clover, who was pure as freshly fallen snow? *Easy.* Smut her beautiful ass out whenever she gave me the chance. But until then, I had to make moves.

"It's late as shit. I should head out and let you get some sleep," I announced.

"You're not too tired to drive, are you?"

I shook my head as I rose to my feet and stretched. "Nah, Lady Luck. I'm good."

"Let me walk you to the door."

We trekked a few feet to the front door and paused. She shifted toward me and swept a few stray hairs behind her ear. "Thank you again for being so cool about the car stuff and then following me home." She paused and took a step closer. "You were the perfect gentleman tonight, Harlan."

"You're always safe with me," I vowed as I brushed the back of my fingertip against her exposed arm.

Her skin was as soft as a blade of grass. I was eager to feel Clover's body pressed against mine. Each time she took a half-step closer to me, my heart jerked against its reins. I was afraid I'd find my lips pressed against hers and my hands in all the right places without her blessing. She'd given me access to her world for the past few hours, but I was still a stranger. I didn't have the right to touch her, to think the dark, dirty thoughts about the sinful things I wanted to do to her heavenly body, but I did them both anyway. I snaked my hand around her throat but didn't apply too much pressure.

A delicate moan escaped her lips as she stood on the tips of her toes. I anchored my gaze to hers before dropping it down to her lips. I wasn't a mothafucka who liked to kiss. It was too intimate. Too personal. I was used to breaking bitches off a lil something like a Kit Kat and sendin' them on their way. It was my system, and I was comfortable with it. But it hadn't even been a full twenty-four hours since I'd been introduced to Clover's aura, and I craved her beautiful ass like my next breath. Then, I kissed her with every ounce of energy I had in me. Since I saw her in the bar, I wanted to make up for all the time I'd spent thinking about doing all the filthy things I wanted to do. Her body melted in my arms and instantly extinguished the fire that had been burning inside me since the night my brother died.

"What the fuck are you doing to me?" I mumbled against her lips. There wasn't a bone in my body that moved. I didn't want the night to end.

"My heart is beating at unhealthy levels," she panted before placing my hand against her chest so I could feel her heart pitter-pattering against her ribcage.

"Mine too."

The room went silent between song transitions, and then "Moment of Your Life" by Brent Faiyaz and Coco Jones came on. *"And I got every other thing that I need and want but you,"* Brent's melodic voice flowed through the speaker.

"I just realized you didn't disconnect your phone," Clover stated, keeping her hand over mine.

"My bad," I replied, slowly running my hand down her chest to the elastic around her shorts.

Clover flashed her lust-filled eyes up at me as Coco crooned in the background, *"Always been a good girl, but I got a bad side. Can I show you, baby?"*

"What you wanna do?" I challenged, putting the ball in her court.

"What do you mean?"

I quickly yanked at the strings on her shorts. "You know what the fuck I mean, Lady Luck," I answered, licking my lips.

She tilted her head to the side. "Well... I was gonna take a shower."

"Say less. Let's go."

I scooped her up in my arms like we were newlyweds and carried her down the hallway, searching for her bedroom. I only had the best intentions when it came to her body and how it needed to be treated when in my hands. I was going to take my sweet time with Clover. She was too irresistible not to. She was going to get blessed by the best. By the end of the night, I was going to have her falling apart, begging for more.

I pushed through the doorway to her bedroom, and my eyes were instantly drawn to her black canopy bed adorned with pink and gray throw pillows and a cozy blanket at the foot. It was the focal piece of her room. A few jarred candles were set on her dresser and nightstands, along with other pink and gray accents throughout. Her room was as stylish and classy as she was.

I laid her down on the bed and snaked my hand up her crop top when she propped herself up on her elbows. "Wait."

I froze. "Tell me to stop, and I'll stop."

"It's not that I want you to stop. I just want to make it clear that this *isn't* a thing I normally do."

"What? Invite strangers over? You told me that off the rip."

"And fuck them," she added. "I don't want you thinking I'm some sort of ho. I haven't had sex in... a *really* long time."

"And why is that?"

She gave me a look before completely sitting up. "Work and no time or desire for an active social life."

"Sounds to me like you're overdue for some good dick then," I replied.

"I was engaged," she blurted out.

My look hardened. The last thing I needed was to have to lay a nigga down for poppin' out her closet or some shit. "*Was?*"

"My fiancé. H-he died of a brain aneurysm two years ago. I haven't dated or slept with anyone since. I haven't wanted to. I was starting to think my pussy was broken or something... until you," she admitted.

My lips lifted on one side. Her honesty was refreshing. She was an innocent little bird with a broken wing. Hearing another piece of her backstory only made me want to nurse her heart and body back to health. "I'm sorry for your loss. I know grief, and it ain't no shit you get through overnight."

"You're right about that. I still wear my ring around my neck," she said, pulling the chain out from underneath her shirt. "You almost touched it when you started going up my shirt, and all these alarms started going off in my brain. I'm sorry for laying all this on you in the heat of the moment. You probably think I'm crazy now."

I shook my head. "The opposite. I'm not trying to rush anything, Lady Luck. If you don't wanna—"

She cut me off. "No. I *want* to. I *need* to. I'm just…"

Before she could complete her sentence, I cut her off with a gentle kiss. "I know you're scared, Lady Luck, and I respect your walls, but I'd be fuckin' lyin' if I said I ain't wanna beat 'em down tonight," I acknowledged softly with a barbaric undertone.

She reached around her neck to unhook the clasp of her necklace and slid it off. I watched as she crawled off the bed and walked over to her dresser to set it there before peeling her cotton tee over her head and tossing it on the floor. Next came her shorts and socks, leaving her in only her lace panties and bra. Her steps minced toward her bathroom before she halted at the door. She cast her sultry gaze over her shoulder to catch mine. "C'mon."

My mouth curved into a smile as I followed her into the bathroom. Clover's face disappeared momentarily while she ducked behind the colorful shower curtain to turn on the water. When she popped back out, she reached up to pull off her glasses when I stopped her.

"Nah. Leave 'em on."

"They're gonna fog up in the shower."

I kept my eyes on her as I stepped closer and slowly slid the green frames off her face before setting them on the edge of the sink. She nibbled on her bottom lip before pulling my lips onto hers. I bundled her into my arms, walking her backward until her back was pressed against the wall beside the shower. She continued kissing me while tugging at the hem of my clothes. I dropped one foot back before pulling my shirt over my head and unbuckling my jeans. She kept her eyes pinned on mine, watching me strip for her before reaching behind her back, unhooking her bra, and shimmying her panties over her hips. I kept my eyes stationed on Clover as she stood in front of me, completely naked. Her body was a work of art with curves in places I only wanted my hands to know. She was already mine in my eyes, and there wasn't a soul walking the earth that would tear us apart.

My hand slipped between her thighs and massaged her swollen clit in slow circles with the tips of my fingers. She was already *so damn* wet. A soft whimper escaped her lips.

"Can I take my time with you tonight?" I murmured against her forehead.

She nodded, and I lifted her right leg onto the edge of the tub before inserting my index and middle fingers deep inside her throbbing pussy in search of her G-spot. Her core clenched around my fingers as I drove them in and out of her warmth in a steady rhythm.

"Fuckkkkkkkk!" she screamed as her body convulsed. She grabbed hold of her left breast and tugged on her nipple. Seconds later, I felt the release of her sweet cream running down my hands.

I eased out of her pussy and stroked my shaft with Clover's wetness while admiring her quivering body. I wanted to give her something never to be forgotten, starting with penning a love letter to her pussy with my tongue. I dropped down on one knee as if I were proposing and embedded myself between her shaking thighs. The butterfly soft kisses I placed followed the curve of her hips as I inched closer to her pink pearl. My tongue was eager to have a one-on-one with the heart of her femininity, but I was determined to take my time and show her what it felt like to be worshipped by a real nigga. Her eyes burned with desire as she looked down at me just as I slid two fingers back inside her. She bolted forward when my tongue joined the party.

Clover moaned. "Oooh my Gooood! Yessss!"

I held both of her hands while my tongue slurped her honeypot and my fingers dipped deeper inside her. She squealed and screamed under the command of my tongue until air could no longer escape her lungs. By that point, I could no longer hold back. I had to be inside her.

The steam fogged the mirror before we stepped inside the warm shower. She placed her palms against the wall as my lips latched onto her neck from behind and I caressed her rounded ass. With my erection standing at full attention, the head of my dick breached her slit from behind. The minute I dipped inside her, I *knew* I was home. The way her pussy hugged my dick was like she'd been made just for me.

"Oooh shit," I growled as the warm water pelted against my back.

I wrapped my hand around her waist and swiped my thumb across her clit while controlling the rhythm of my stroke. Clover's feverish moans and innocent squeals every time I thrusted inside her or pulled her hair drove me wild. I couldn't get enough of her. After twenty minutes of fucking in the shower, Clover shut off the water and we stepped out. The cold air made the hair on my body stand on end as goosebumps pebbled my skin. I pulled her slippery body to mine before cupping her ass and lifting her. She locked her arms around my neck, clinging to me as I led us to finish what we'd started in the bathroom to her canopy bed. Our dripping bodies slid against each other as I fell against the bed on my back. Clover's eyes flickered with desire as she mounted me, begging me to sink back into her sweet heat. I cupped her ass cheeks as she eased down on top of me. Her forehead puckered as I filled her to the brim.

"Oooh shit," she hissed, sucking in air through her teeth.

I gripped her hips, determined to make her scream my name and cum until she was ready to pass out. "Mmm, shit, just like that."

Clover relentlessly moved her hips against my erection, sinking her nails into the meat around my shoulders as she bucked and bounced. Her brown eyes glinted with desire. I was certain there wasn't a bitch walking God's green earth that was badder than she was. I reached up to wrap my hand around her throat while placing my thumb in her mouth to suck on. She flashed her eyes up to the ceiling while calling on the Lord. God was the *only* one who could save her from me.

"Holy fuck, I'm about to cum!" she screamed.

"That's it, baby girl, wet this fuckin' dick up," I growled before slipping a finger inside her tight asshole. Clover's pussy was a wave pool, and I savored each second I got to play in her waterpark.

"Oh my God! Oh my God! Yessss!"

Tears filled her eyes as she came. A devious grin spread across my face when I felt the creamy mess between us. I flipped her over onto her back, keeping my shit buried deep inside her warmth.

Adhering to my position change, Clover's legs enveloped my waist as she serenaded me with her needy moans. Missing her sweet lips, I kissed her greedily. Her hands caressed my tattooed back, scraping at my skin. I pried my lips away from hers and smushed her breasts together before rolling my tongue across her rock-hard nipples and sucking on them hungrily.

"You're so fuckin' beautiful," I whispered against her cocoa buttery soft skin.

Clover's smooth, toned legs rested on my shoulders as I choked her with one hand and thumbed her clit with the other. Neither of us broke eye contact.

"Yes! Yes! Just like that! Don't stop, Harlan! Please, don't stop!" Clover begged. Her lower lip trembled with each moan.

Picking up the pace, I planked over her while my length went in and out of her until my dick turned white with her nut.

The muscle in my jaw twitched. "Shit," I groaned, feeling the building anticipation of my climax.

My lips drew back in a snarl as I quickened my stroke, fucking her harder and faster until I came. I slammed my eyes shut as my body jerked and quaked inside her. "Fuckkkkkkkk!"

It was the most euphoric nut I'd ever had in my life. The feeling was indescribable. Her pussy had the power to end wars *and* start them. I rolled over onto my back, panting heavily. A few minutes later, I got up to go into the bathroom to grab my clothes when my cell phone spilled out of my pocket. I picked it up to see four missed calls and a dozen texts from Chop. After my club member won his race, two bikers from a rival MC gang, the Diablo Disciples, pulled up and started firing off rounds, creating chaos. His bike got sprayed with bullets, causing the engine to blow up. They fled the scene before the police and paramedics arrived.

"*Fuck*," I hissed, shooting up to my feet.

"Is everything okay?"

"Nah. I gotta go."

Her brows downturned. "Harlan, what's wrong?"

"I can't talk about it right now, Clover! I gotta go, *aight*? I'll call you!" I promised as I rushed to put on the rest of my clothes and raced out the door.

CLOVER

ne week later.

Harlan had been living rent-free inside my mind since the night we'd spent together. Any free space I had in my thoughts were reserved for him. It was all Harlan, all the time, twenty-four-seven. He was the first man I'd let get close enough to get a whiff of my honeypot since Lorenzo's death, and it was the best decision I'd ever made. At least, I *thought* it was. Although he'd left my pussy tender and battered in the best possible ways, I hadn't heard from him since he fled my place in such a hurry in the wee hours of the morning. I would randomly find myself staring at my phone, its screen dark, waiting for him. No messages. No calls. Just silence. A week had passed since our intimate encounter, and I couldn't shake the gnawing uncertainty. Had he lost interest already? Was our overwhelming connection only for the night and destined to fizzle out?

As challenging as it was, I was determined to put him out of my mind long enough to get through my interview. There was an open position for a travel ER nurse, and I wanted it. My wandering spirit had me ready for a change of scenery and a pay increase. I'd been searching for a fresh start for the past few months, and when I discovered the open travel ER nurse position from a reputable staffing agency, I jumped at the chance. All I had to do was showcase my expertise and why I was the best candidate for the job. I arrived at the hospital two hours before my shift, nerves tingling as I approached the elevators toward the third floor. I shook hands with the recruiter as she led me into a quiet, unoccupied conference room with sunlight filtering through the blinds. I drew in a deep breath.

"Thank you for meeting with me today, Miss Baldwin. I'm Kathy Sears, one of the recruiters with U.S. Travel Nurses. How are you today?" she asked as she extended her hand.

I returned the gesture before introducing myself confidently. Her kind eyes made me feel at ease as I settled into my chair across from her. "I'm excited to meet with you today."

"Great," she replied, glancing over a printed copy of my resume. "Your resume is impressive. Can you tell me something about yourself that I won't find on the paper in front of me, starting with why you want to become a travel nurse?"

I drew in a deep breath while replaying her question in my head before answering. "I've worked as an ED nurse for some time now. Anybody who works in the ED knows the job can be just as stressful as it is unpredictable, but I tend to thrive in chaos. Plus, I've always enjoyed traveling, so I figure why not mesh the two things together?"

Ms. Sears cleared her throat. "I've been a registered nurse for over thirty years. Of those thirty, I traveled for twelve of them. I've talked to hundreds of nurses. I know this job is hard, Ms. Baldwin. Becoming a traveling nurse only makes it harder. You're a fish out of water in a new place, which could be exciting, depending on your personality. You're away from the people you love for months at a time. You've got to allow time for the people on your new team to trust you. So, if traveling is the only reason you want to do this, I'm afraid this may not be the position for you."

My smile dimmed as I sighed. "You're right, and if possible, I'd like to modify my initial answer."

"Why?"

"Because it wasn't the truth, well, not the whole truth anyway."

"It's not?"

I sighed. "No, ma'am. The truth is, I've been looking for a change ever since my fiancé passed away."

She lowered her head. "I'm sorry for your loss."

"Thank you. Don't get me wrong, the opportunity to travel still excites me. But beyond that, for the first time in my life, I want to experience the freedom of choosing my path instead of life choosing for me. I want to work in diverse healthcare settings. I want to learn and soak up as much knowledge as I can. I... I've been walking around half-empty for far too long, Ms. Sears. I want to feel fulfilled again. Becoming a travel nurse is the first of many steps in the right direction."

She shot me a warm smile. "I like that answer a lot better."

"Thanks. Me too."

"Tell me how you handle workplace stress."

I paused again, hoping to hit it out of the park on my first try, the second go-round. "What works best for me when things are crazy, which is every day, if I'm being honest, is to focus on handling one task at a time. I'm a very detail-oriented person. I use checklists, to-do lists, among other things to keep myself organized and ensure my patients receive the best care. Additionally, I've never been afraid to lean on my team. We have a *great* team of nurses here, and I can only pray I have the chance to be on similar well-rounded teams at any other healthcare facility I work at in the future."

"I see you've worked as a nurse here for over two years. Tell me about your craziest night in the ER."

"Every night comes with its own set of crazy, but if I have to pick, I'd say it was last winter. There was a blizzard, and you know, when big winter storms hit, the ER gets slammed with a plethora of orthopedic fractures from people slipping on black ice. That night, in particular, I helped treat two drunk college kids who were riding hoverboards through the snow, making TikTok videos, hoping to go viral. One fractured his left wrist, and the other injured his hip so badly that he ended up needing surgery. Needless to say, liquor, snow, and motorized skateboards don't mix."

She chuckled. "Surely a recipe for disaster."

I laughed with her. "For sure."

"As you may already know, ER travel nurses are in high demand. We have open positions at hospitals in Washington, D.C., Hawaii, and New York. Each contract is about thirteen weeks and would land you anywhere between twenty-six hundred to three thousand dollars a week," she explained.

"And the shifts?"

"Some are to be determined, while most are four, twelve-hour days or three, depending on the location. Is that something you're comfortable with?"

I bobbed my head. "Yes. I'm used to working twelve-hour shifts regularly. The hours aren't a problem. Getting used to the time change might be, but not the hours," I said with a soft chuckle.

"Awesome. Do you have any additional questions for me?"

"I do. What are some of the benefits your company offers traveling nurses?"

"Great question. For one, we know you want a good, livable wage. Our company strives hard to be competitive and offers one-of-a-kind benefits for our nurses like free mental health check-ins with licensed therapists nationwide, student loan reimbursement, and bonuses for exemplary work."

I smiled. "Sounds good."

"Is there anything else you'd like to ask before we wrap up?"

"No. Not that I can think of right now."

She stood to her feet to shake my hand again. "Thank you for your time today, Ms. Baldwin. I'll be in touch soon."

"Thank you." I beamed. "I'm looking forward to it."

By the end of the interview, I was one hundred percent sold on becoming a travel nurse. Would it be an adjustment? Sure. But it was an adjustment I was ready to take on under my terms. I'd been dying for an opportunity to leave Chicago behind since Lorenzo's death, and a new job in a new place felt like the right move. Besides, it seemed like the nurse-patient ratios would be better, and with all the possibilities of new travel, I hoped I wouldn't feel burnt out after a few months. I shook Kathy's hand once more before turning to leave. I had over two years of emergency room experience, my record was spotless, and I attended medical confer-ences instead of concerts for fun. As far as I was concerned, I had that interview in the bag. All I had to do was sit back and wait for her call.

———

While working the evening surge, I was about to administer medication to a patient with chronic pain when Gwen, one of my fellow nurses on my shift, called out to me. "Hey, Clover. There's someone in bed seven asking for you by name," she informed me.

My brows downturned. "*Me*? Who is it?"

She shrugged before looking down at the clipboard in her hand. "Wouldn't give me a name."

"Can you take these Motrin tablets to the man in bed two? He's demanding opioids, but he's got strict restrictions in his chart."

"Sure."

"Thanks."

I marched toward the curtain and snatched it back to see Luther "Lux" Dorsey, Lorenzo's older brother, sitting on the gurney's edge with his hand over his bleeding shoulder. There were bloodstains on his calloused, sandy brown hands and shirt. He was trapped under my narrow-eyed scrutiny as my eyes snaked along his scruffy beard and long dreads with honey-colored tips pulled into a messy high bun. He always wore a permanent scowl, but I knew the pain behind his hard brown eyes and the tattoos etched into his bloodied skin. One look at him and I knew exactly why he'd requested me. We were connected beyond symp-toms and diagnoses. I sighed, hoping to shake away the emotional residue so that I could do my job properly.

"Lux? What the *fuck* happened you to?" I hissed before snatching the curtain closed behind me.

"Clo, wassup, sis?"

My brows remained raised. "What happened to you, Lux?"

"I had a lil run in with the wrong mothafuckas, that's all. It's just a graze. All I need you to do is stitch a nigga up."

"Let me get this straight. You were shot, and you want me to slap a

Band-Aid over a bullet wound and send you on your way? Do I need to page psych and have your ass evaluated?" I snapped while folding my arms across my chest.

He sucked his teeth. "C'mon, Clo. Don't be like that. You know I can't be around all these doctors and shit, and you know I don't do cops. I came here for you, and you only."

"How'd you even know I was on shift tonight?"

"It's you, Clo. You barely leave this bitch." He snorted.

I rolled my eyes skyward. "Whatever. You lucky you're like family to me."

He smirked. "See, I knew you'd always have my back, sis."

"Wait here while I get some supplies."

I pulled the curtain shut behind me before dipping into a nearby supply room to grab some gauze and other medical supplies to stitch him up in secrecy. I hadn't seen Lux in at least a year, if not longer. He'd been running in the streets as long as I'd known him, and he still hadn't stopped by the looks of things. I loved him like family, which always made his reckless behavior easy to dismiss. Seeing him again stirred up a cocktail of emotions inside me. On one hand, I was happy to know that he was still alive and semi-well, but on the other, it was like a blast from the past that I wasn't sure how to handle. I headed back after grabbing everything I needed.

"Here, take these. They'll help with the pain," I said, passing him a small cup with two pills in it. "It was all I could get."

He reached out to take the cup and tossed the pain meds down his throat before washing them down with some water. "How you been, sis?"

"I've been okay. I would ask how you've been, but I think we both see you're livin' life by the seat of your damn pants," I judged.

He snickered. "Chill. It's just a lil gunshot graze."

"Your ass needs to slow down, Lux."

"Slow down? Shit, I'm just gettin' started, sis."

"You're all done. Remember to change the bandages every day and make sure you keep your wound clean, or else you'll be right back here with an infection."

He stood to his feet, allowing his six-foot frame to tower over me as he extended his good arm. "Thank you."

"You're welcome. Now, *please*, be careful."

He kissed my forehead. "I love you, Clo. You know you'll always be la familia. I got you with anything you need."

"What I need is for you to slow down, like I said. I mean, damn, Lux, you're not tired of living the fast life yet?"

"Live fast, die hard, right?" he inquired with a devilish smirk.

I shook my head. His response made it clear that my words were being brushed to the side, so I gave up. "I'ma keep your ass in prayer."

He cheesed. "Bet. I need all the good juju I can get out in these streets. You still got the same number?"

"Yeah, I do."

"Good. I'll hit you up the next time I need your services."

"I truly hope that's no time soon."

"Neva know," he replied before swiping his worn leather jacket off the chair and disappearing behind the curtain.

———

I spent my next day off joined at the hip with Quintessa all day while trying not to focus on the fact that I still hadn't heard from Harlan. We met at a cozy cafe with large, sunlit windows and sipped on cappuccinos and fragrant herbal teas while discussing everything from work escapades to our personal lives. As badly as I wanted to dish and tell her every single juicy detail about my night with Harlan, I was too caught up in my head about the uncertainty of it all to bring it up.

By mid-morning, Q and I were wandering through the farmer's market, sifting through stalls filled with colorful produce, artisanal cheeses, and handmade jewelry and crafts by local vendors. We sampled fresh, juicy strawberries while picking ingredients for a future cooking escapade. All I could do was pray it didn't go bad by the time I spent more than four and a half minutes in my kitchen preparing a meal. I wanted to learn how to do fancy shit in the kitchen, like make pasta from scratch or master the art of sushi rolling. I had goals. After the farmer's market, we settled into a quaint bistro with fairy lights and cute rustic charm to sip wine and order our favorite comfort foods.

"We should toast," Quintessa suggested.

"To what?"

She shrugged. "I don't know, friendship, a bomb ass relaxing day off?"

"Mmm, yes! All of the above. I don't know about you, but I definitely needed today. The only thing left is to take a relaxing bubble bath when I get home."

"What we need is another club night without my sister's drunk ass ruining the night."

I rolled my eyes. "Girl, don't get me started about that night."

"What do you mean? You never did tell me what happened after we left your place. Did you invite the cutie from the bar upstairs?"

I groaned. It was only a matter of time before the news bubbled up and spilled out of me. "I did."

"And?"

"And... it was everything I needed."

Her brows shot toward her forehead. "What?"

I smacked my lips. "I swear I was not trying to make a big deal out of this, but—"

She cut me off. "Hold up! Did you let him hit it on the first night?"

I squinted my gaze before nodding. "I did."

"How was it?"

"Delectable," I responded with a chef's kiss.

Quintessa squealed with excitement. "Ooooh shit! I know you fuckin' lying! Tell me everything! How long? How wide? How was the stroke? Did he lick it before he stuck it?" she blabbed.

I cackled. She truly tickled me, making me feel even more at ease. "He did all of the above. He took his time with me. And that tongue and those hands, mmm, mmm, good."

"Yum! So what's next? When will little Miss Clover be on his menu again?"

My smile faded when thoughts about the uncertain future crept into the forefront of my brain. "I-I don't know," I answered as my shoulders rose and fell.

"I'm confused. You just sat here in my face and said the dick was bomb, right?"

"Yeah, so?"

"So?"

"He hasn't hit me up, okay?" I confessed with a sigh.

"What do you mean he hasn't hit you up?"

"We spent all night together, and then after we fucked, he checked his phone and ran out of my place like the damn floor was lava. I haven't heard from him since, and that was like a week ago. So, it's over. It's totally over, right?"

Quintessa rolled her eyes. "Only if you want it to be."

"I don't."

"Then hit him up!" she insisted.

"You don't think that looks... y'know, *desperate*?"

"You said the D was delectable, right?"

"Yeah."

"So what's the problem?"

"I don't even know what to say."

"How about, hey, wassup? Hope you and that dick are blessed, Black, and highly favored. When you gon' come over and break my back again?"

I belted out a laugh. "You're a whole mess, do you know that?"

"Hey, I'm just being honest. Life is too short not to get good dick every chance you can."

"Ugh. I just don't understand why he hasn't said anything. What if he thought I was bad or something? I mean, it had been a very long time."

Quintessa's head did a 180. "You're way too much in your head for this. Drink some more wine so your ass loosens up some more."

"Fine! Okay, okay. I'm going to do it!" I insisted while picking my phone up from the table.

Me: *Hey,* I texted.

I kept my eyes glued to the screen as the three ellipses populated. I exhaled the moment they disappeared. I hadn't even realized I'd been holding my breath. Seconds later, my phone vibrated in my palm.

"Oh shit, he's calling me. He's calling right now!"

"Stop being a pussy and answer it!" Quintessa encouraged before gulping down her last bit of red wine.

I huffed before jabbing my thumb over the accept button and pressing the phone to my ear. "H-hello?" I answered before clearing my throat.

"Wassup, Lady Luck?"

"Harlan, h-hey. How are you?"

"I'm aight, and you?" I quizzed, hoping he'd shed some light on why he'd gone ghost.

"We should link up soon. You got a nigga missin' you and shit."

"Missing me?" I questioned. "From how you darted out of my apartment so fast, I would've thought the opposite."

"Nah. That had nothin' to do with you."

"You sure about that?" I quizzed, partially turned off.

I'd hoped when the time came for him to answer, he would've been more straight up than vague.

"Positive. Let me make it up to you," he insisted.

"What exactly did you have in mind?"

"A date."

"A date?"

"Yeah."

"When?"

"Tonight, if you're free."

My eyes bugged wide as I shot them toward Quintessa. I mouthed the words *he wants to meet tonight,* and she nodded. I cleared my throat. "Uh, yeah. I think I can move some things around. What did you have in mind?"

"Tell me something you'd like to do, and I'll make it happen."

"Surprise me," I told him. "Just make sure it's something competitive but fun."

"Bet. I'll text you, aight?"

"Okay," I replied before ending the call.

Harlan's call had ignited a spark inside me that triggered visions of him. My thoughts danced between our stolen glances during our first encounter at the bar, to our whispered secrets the first night we spent together, and the brush of his soft lips against my longing skin. I was enamored with how delicately he treated my body. Our chemistry was undeniable, like two yearning celestial bodies pulled together by gravity.

But now, as I mentally prepared for our second meeting, a wave of doubt rolled in like a silent thief sent to steal my joy. *What if it's awkward? What if the spark is gone? Maybe I should cancel. I'll blame it on a sudden work emergency in the ED. He'll understand that.*

I was trapped inside my head and willing to do almost anything to avoid facing the possibility of disappointment. But then, hope seeped in through the cracks of my mind. I remembered the way his hearty laughter had filled the air between us as we sat on my couch, learning each other, how he'd unknowingly traced constellations on my skin. I recalled the way he looked at me—a blend of desire and devotion, as if I was a goddess or the universe itself. I replayed his voice—the intensity that sent shivers down my spine. I could almost smell the lingering scent of his cologne, feel the warmth of his fingertips against the small of my back. *No. I won't sabotage this. Not before it begins.*

———

Hours after the sun went down, I arrived at the bowling alley to meet Harlan. My nerves tingled with anticipation. We were doing everything ass backward in my eyes, dating *after* sex, but I was still excited to see him again. I couldn't read him through the phone, but I was damn sure going to get a better feel for him on our date. It was one thing to see how a person acted behind closed doors, but seeing how they conducted themselves in public was different. After checking my reflection in the visor mirror to fluff out my long hair and touch up my matte burgundy lipstick, I texted him to let him know I'd arrived. Seconds later, I heard the loud rumbling of an engine nearby. I twisted my neck to see a man on a black and red motorcycle pull up beside me. He killed the engine before pulling his helmet off his head to reveal himself. It was Harlan. I stepped out to greet him with a wide smile on my face. I couldn't hide my giddiness if I tried. We exchanged warm smiles before he extended his arms to pull me into a hug and kiss my cheek.

"You look and smell amazing," he complimented, surveying me from head to toe.

I wore a black spaghetti-strapped tank top with black skinny jeans. My burgundy leather jacket, black boots, and hoop earrings completed my outfit.

"Thank you. I feel overdressed. I didn't know where we were going."

"Nah. You look perfect to me."

I smirked as I gave him a onceover. "You looking fly yourself."

He wore loose-fit denim jeans, black boots, and a designer hoodie with the LV monogram stamped all over it underneath his leather jacket.

"What made you pick bowling for our first date?"

"I know you were probably expecting a nigga to take you to a five-star restaurant or something, but you said you wanted competition. Ain't shit to compete over at a restaurant unless you the chef. But we can go somewhere else if you want."

My face gleamed with excitement. "No. I haven't been bowling in so long, so I'll suck the first few rounds, but I'm sure I'll find my stride. I'm excited!"

"Okay then. Let's see whatchu got."

We stepped inside, and the sound of rolling balls, cracking pins, and laughter filled the air. I looked around at the spacious area with sixteen lanes, a game area, a snack bar, and a shoe rental station. I hadn't been inside a bowling alley in years, but the casual atmosphere put my nerves at ease.

Harlan's large hand swallowed mine as I followed him toward the lanes. "Which lane you want, Lady Luck? Lucky number seven or something else?"

"Seven is cool with me."

We approached the seventh lane bathed in neon lights before slipping on our rented bowling shoes with quirky colors. We grabbed our bowling balls before the friendly competition ignited. Harlan came out the gate, rolling strikes and spares while I had a gutter ball every other turn. Nonetheless, we cheered each other on, and I made sure to do a goofy victory dance every time I hit *at least* one pin.

"Yo, I'm hungry. What about you?" Harlan asked between frames.

"Me too. Let's hit the snack bar."

We ordered nachos, two soft pretzels, and a basket of fries to share before returning to our lane to dig in. Usually, I would've watched what and how I ate around a man initially, but Harlan made me feel comfortable in my skin. I didn't have to hide or put on airs for him.

"Yo, these nachos are good as fuck," he said mid-bite. "You wanna try one?"

I bobbed my head. "Hit me."

He fed me a bite from across the table before playfully wiping away the drop of cheese lingering on my chin. "Good, right?"

"Uh, yes. Yum! I should've gotten some for myself."

"You can have whatever you want."

I smiled. "Don't give me a pass to eat up all your food because I will."

He chuckled as his eyes devoured me. "You sound like me. I can eat thirds and *still* be hungry."

I crossed my legs under the table, squeezing my thighs together. "Oh yeah?"

"Yeah," he confirmed with a swift dip of his chin.

Harlan leaned in close enough to breathe in the same air as me, and the noise of the alley instantly faded. The dim glow of the neon lights cast a romantic aura around him. Suddenly, it was only the two of us in the room. Before my lips could meet his, my phone vibrated in my back pocket. I looked down to see Lux's name and number across the screen before quickly pressing ignore. As soon as I tapped the button, I started to wonder if he called because his wound had gotten infected or he'd gone somewhere and gotten his ass shot at again. So I texted him.

Me: *I'm out with some friends. Are you good?*

Lux: *Everything good, sis. I'm just makin' sure you still had my number locked in. Be safe.*

I breathed a sigh of relief before liking his message and turning my attention back to Harlan. "I'm sorry."

"Everything good?" he probed, eyeing me suspiciously.

I nodded. "Yup, all good."

"You sure? You looked a lil panicked over there for a second."

"It was nothing. C'mon, the last frame is up. It's your turn," I told him, hoping he'd drop it.

The last frame arrived, and Harlan stepped up to grab his ball. I watched him take a deep breath before releasing the ball down the lane. The ball rolled down the lane rapidly, colliding with all but three pins. He cleared them after his second roll and got a spare. He turned to me with a triumphant grin as I clapped my hands.

"It's yo' turn. No pressure," he commented with a snicker.

I could feel his eyes on me as I lined up my roll. I slowly twisted my neck over my shoulder to see his eyes stationed on me. "You scared?" he called out with a snarky smirk.

"Shut up!" I snapped back before turning around to refocus.

I pulled in a breath before drawing my arm back and releasing the ball. I stared in anticipation as the ball raced down the lane. To my surprise, every single pin scattered on the first roll. Strike! I immediately broke out into a victory dance before Harlan approached me and twirled me in his strong arms.

"Did you see that? Tell me you fucking saw that!" I squealed with excitement.

"Hell yeah, I saw that shit!"

"Holy shit! That was my first strike ever!"

"Glad I got to experience it witchu," Harlan replied, keeping my body pinned to his.

He hadn't been lying the night we met when he told me with him was the safest place I could be. Being with Harlan felt familiar, yet it had all the bells and whistles of a shiny new relationship. With him, a part of me felt like I was home. I hated comparing everything I felt for him to what I shared with Lorenzo. A small part of me felt guilty for taking the necklace off. I hadn't put it back on since I'd slept with Harlan. It was almost as if being with him broke me out of the grieving mold I'd been resting in since Lorenzo's passing.

Zo and I first crossed paths at a hole-in-the-wall antique shop tucked away from all the city's chaos on the west side. I was a young stargazer with aspirations of becoming an astronomer before I got the calling to become a nurse. I wandered through the aisles filled with vintage knick-knacks and dusty artifacts, tracing the constellations engraved into a timeworn globe. When our eyes met, it was as if our hearts intersected. He smiled, and my heart stopped... so did time. I'd never seen anyone with such beautiful brown eyes. We drew to each other like magnets, unable to resist the pull. I got close enough to see the constellation of freckles across his nose that looked like the Three Leaps of the Gazelle and fell in love.

We dated for four years before he popped the question. On paper, he checked all my parents' boxes. Zo wasn't perfect, but his eyes held so much love for me. I never had to question where I stood with him. There was no doubt in my mind that we'd spend the rest of our lives together. I thought the stolen kisses, uncontrollable laughter, and stargazing sessions would last forever, but life had other plans.

"You ready to go for round two?" Harlan quizzed, snapping me out of my daze.

I dipped my chin. "Yup. Let's do it!"

———

Our evening came to a close at the end of the second game. Of course, he whupped my ass, rolling damn near a perfect game, but I had fun regardless. We returned our bowling shoes and stepped outside, laughing.

"Thank you for tonight. I haven't had that much fun in a long time," I told him as we approached my car.

"I'm glad I could show you a good time. You took that L like a G." He snickered.

I rolled my eyes toward the starlit sky. "Or maybe I'm just so nice I let you win," I retorted with a smirk before casting my attention down to the debris scattering across the pavement.

"You been lookin' like you've had somethin' you wanted to get off your chest all night. Wassup?" he asked, tilting his head to the side.

I shook my head. "No. It's nothing. We've had such a great night. I don't wanna ruin things."

"Get it off your chest, Lady Luck."

A breath eased out before I spoke. "I guess I'm just wondering why it took me reaching out to you for this to happen again. I mean, how am I to know this wasn't just some post-pussy pity date?"

Harlan willed his legs toward me, narrowing the space between us.

He was close enough to feel the jackhammering of my heart through my chest. He hooked his hand around my throat before he kissed me like I'd never been kissed before. His lips were warm and soft, and his tongue wasn't invasive or overbearing like most men's. It wasn't a Hollywood moment with a dip and an ankle pop, but the way his hand gripped my ass as he kissed me made it perfect enough to melt *all* my insecurities away. My pussy started doing all sorts of crazy things whenever I was in his possession. Whatever had stolen his attention away from me that night was in the past. All that mattered was the here and now.

"Did that feel like pity to you?" he challenged after slowly breaking the kiss.

His words pricked my heart. "Not at all," I whispered against his lips before stealing another kiss. I craved more of him. I wasn't ready for it to end.

"I've wanted to do that since I pulled up beside you," he admitted as his hand slowly fell from my neck.

I caught his hand and pulled it up to my lips, kissing the skull tattoo on the back of his hand. "Why didn't you?"

"Because I'm tryin' my best *not* to disrespect you, Lady Luck."

"What if I want you to... in my bed or wherever else you want me?" I taunted before dragging my eyes up to meet his as I sucked his finger.

"Mmm, shit," he growled while squeezing my ass. "Say less. I'll follow you home."

He backed away with an impressive bulge in his pants before he tossed his leg over his motorcycle and started the engine. I quickly unlocked my car and got inside. Just the thought of having Harlan inside me again made my panties flood. I couldn't think of a better way to end our first date than with my legs in the air and Harlan between my thighs.

HARLAN

Clover and I lay side by side on her soft mattress as our fingers brushed against each other. The air smelled of unforgettable sex and sweat. I licked my lips, reminiscing on our most recent session. Her pussy tasted like holy water, and I could've let her baptize me in that shit all night long if she wanted to. I swiveled my head, studying her beautiful profile. The moonlight traced the curve of her cheek, casting shadows that danced in her sienna-brown eyes. She shifted closer, allowing the warmth of her naked body to seep into my skin.

The scent of Clover's vanilla scented body clung to my skin for hours after I left her presence that first night. It was a constant reminder of our time together. I'd done things to her body that defied logic and gravity. Something about that night had unraveled me, leaving a nigga feeling vulnerable and exposed. Two things I didn't fuck with. I'd always prided myself on being the hardened, unyielding type, the kind of nigga who never let emotions tether me. But then Clover walked into my life, and instantly, all my certainties about what I thought I knew blurred. But what choice did I have? Her smile haunted my thoughts, the way her laughter danced across the room, brightening up the darkest of days. Her brown eyes were a blend of warmth and solace.

And her kiss? Her lips had branded my heart on contact, burning through layers of distrust. I'd fallen for her like a fiery meteor plummeting to Earth.

Before her, I would have done anything to avoid exposing my heart. But the night we met, I felt this unexplainable pull, a gravitational force that drew me straight to her. I couldn't run. Not from her. Not from us or whatever we could be. Clover was the only woman I was willing to face the unknown for, even if it meant losing myself in the unchartered territories of her heart and mine.

"The moon is beautiful tonight," she whispered as she pointed to the view outside her bedroom window.

"Mmhm."

"Do you believe in astrology?"

"What you mean? Like, stars and zodiac signs and shit?"

"Yeah, something like that."

"Nah. You?"

Her fingers traced patterns on my palm. "I do. I've always had half my head in reality and the other in the clouds. I guess that's why I've always been drawn to constellations," she admitted. "What's your sign?"

"I'm a Taurus."

"Hmmm, a Taurus man, huh?"

"Somethin' wrong with that?"

"No. It means you're loyal, committed to the people you love, and sensual."

I smirked. "That sounds about right."

"It also means you're stubborn, not big on commitment, and possessive."

"You ain't wrong about that either. Since you already seem to know so much about me, what's your sign? What red flags should I be looking out for witchu?" I quizzed, turning the question back on her.

"I'm a Pisces, which means I'm compassionate, generous, creative, and adaptable. I tend to go with the flow of life most of the time. But, if I had to identify my red flags, I'd probably have to say I can be overly sensitive at times, a bit insecure, and indecisive."

"I can deal with all that shit."

"You say that so confidently."

"That's because I am. I ain't like no other nigga you ever had, Lady Luck."

A light laugh fell from her lips. "Since you've dubbed me Lady Luck, I need to give you a nickname too. Do you already go by anything?"

"All my niggas call me Harlan the Heartless."

"Well, I'm not calling you that, although I am curious about how you got it."

"It pretty much speaks for itself. I've been heartless toward my enemies all my life, and I've never been big on commitment until you."

"Me? What made me different?"

"Everything," I told her.

From the way Clover's body seemed to fit mine like a hand in a glove to how she bravely made the first move and reached out to me, Clover had made it clear her heart and her pussy were mine for the taking. My lost soul had found solace in her. I wasn't about to let that go. I hesitated before drawing in a deep breath. "Maybe it can have a different meaning now."

"Like what?"

"I'm only heartless because I got you holdin' onto it for me."

Her delicate fingers traced the contours of my face and our lips met before she could reply. It was a gentle collision of vulnerability and lust. It wasn't just a kiss; it was a promise. A promise to always protect her, put her first, and take my time while mapping out the constellations of her heart. My hands roamed all over her body's peaks and valleys as my tongue explored her mouth. I wondered if she could sense my vulnerability. Would she know from my kiss that I'd spent sleepless nights deciphering her texts, analyzing every word?

"Tell me something no one else knows about you," Clover whispered against my lips after breaking the kiss.

"I blame myself for my brother's death," I admitted before even thinking about what was coming out of my mouth.

Clover's eyes sought out mine as she sat up on her elbows. "Why?"

I instantly regretted my words. "I don't know why I said that shit."

"Is it the truth?"

"Yeah."

"Then, I'm glad you said it. All I wanna know now is why you feel that way."

"My brother, Harlow, was killed three months ago, and I still haven't found out who did it. Every breath they take is disrespect to my brother and our family."

"So you feel responsible for your brother's death because you haven't gotten justice for him?"

I dipped my chin. "Ever since we were kids, all he ever wanted to do was protect me. And the chance I had to be there for him, I wasn't."

"Do you mind if I ask what happened to him?"

"He was on his way out of town when I called him because one of our stash spots got hit. I told him I had everything under control, but he decided to come back and check things out for himself. That's when his car got shot up. I got the traffic camera footage from the police and watched three motorcycles pull up on him at a red light and shoot up his car. He might still be here if I'd never called him and just handled it like I said I would."

"I'm so sorry for your loss, Harlan."

"Thank you."

"You know it's not your fault, right?"

Her comment softened the harshness of my expression. "I hear you, and I appreciate it, but that don't change how I feel about it."

There'd been a mountain of chaos weighing me down ever since Low took his last breath. I hadn't spoken about how I felt to anyone, not even Chop. Yet, I was laid up with Clover, spilling all my deepest secrets as if she were my confidant. There was so much damn darkness within me—past regrets, unhealed wounds, and battle scars. But whenever I was with her, I could finally see the light.

"I know what it's like to lose someone close to you," she stated without going further.

I wasn't going to press her on the matter. She'd already told me about the death of her fiancé, and I knew death was a touchy subject for most people. "Since you know all about the stars and moons and shit, what do you think happens to us after we die?"

"You mean, like, Heaven and Hell, or something deeper?"

I shrugged. "You tell me. I've seen the darkest parts of life, pure hell on earth. I don't even know if I believe Hell exists. Can't no fuckin' place be worse than this."

"Personally, I think our souls are eternal. I read somewhere once that when you die, your soul can travel down one of two paths. One leads to the afterlife, like Heaven or Hell. The other leads to reincarnation. Either way, your spirit is continuing," she explained.

"So, by your logic, that's why it feels like I've been here with you before? Because I met your beautiful ass in a past life?"

Clover smirked. "You, too, huh?"

A soft laugh huffed through my nostrils. "Oh. So, it's not just me?"

She swung her head in a no. "Not at all."

"Because the way you got a nigga spillin' secrets and gettin' all deep is crazy. As you can see, a nigga's soul is still under development."

"I'm glad you can be yourself with me. It's a pleasure to watch you bloom, Harlan."

Unbeknownst to her, Clover's gentle demeanor had been enticing my stubborn ass to get in touch with my soft side more often than not. I didn't open up to anyone, and yet, every time I got around her, I was spilling another secret about myself. As much as I didn't like it, I appreciated the safe space her presence provided. For that, she'd always have my loyalty.

"I got a question for you now," I stated.

"Shoot."

"Why'd you think our date earlier was out of pity?"

She looked regretful. "I shouldn't have said that."

"You should've if it's how you felt. Is it?"

"Kind of. I mean, yeah, I did for the first two seconds of the night. But then it went away."

I arched a questioning brow. "You sure about that?"

"I just wanted to know where you were, what happened, maybe even a good morning text the day after. But when I got nothing from you, my mind started drawing its own conclusions."

"I didn't wanna leave you like that, but I have responsibilities."

"Responsibilities to what or to whom?" she quizzed.

"You remember when I told you I was the president of The Spades?"

"Yeah."

"Well, the night we met, a couple of members from a rival motor-cycle gang, the Diablo Disciples, shot up my crew member's ride. The engine on Zyon's bike blew up in the parking lot. Those pussy ass niggas put him in the hospital and fled the scene before the cops got there. So I had to get to the hospital and check on my people."

Clover scoffed before covering her face with her hands. "I'm so stupid. "I'm sorry."

"For what?"

"For questioning you in the first place. When you left so quickly, my insecurities started eating me alive, and I automatically assumed the worst."

"What did you think happened?"

Her lean shoulders rose and fell. "I figured you were married and had to get home to your wife or something."

I deaded that notion. "Nah. The only person I wanna race home to is you."

"I know I probably shouldn't like how that sounds, but I do," she admitted. "I don't know how to describe whatever this is between us, but I haven't felt this way about anyone in a long time. You give me butterflies like I'm thirteen again, Harlan."

I kissed her deeply, allowing my lips to say things I couldn't find the words for as I cradled her. We embraced each other like gravity plotted to keep our bodies fused like s'mores.

"But on a serious note, I know I told you that you're safe whenever you're with me, but I wanna make sure you know who I fuck with in this city and who I don't. The Diablo Disciples are a bunch of savage mothafuckas. We've been beefing over drug territory in this city for years. If you see one when I'm not around, you get out of wherever you are, and you call me, aight?"

"How would I know if I ran into one?"

"They'll be wearing their insignia on their jackets or maybe even have a tattoo of a skull crying red tears."

She bobbed her head. "Okay."

———

As the night deepened, we shared stories of childhood memories and fears and laughed until tears blurred our vision. Being with Clover made me realize that intimacy wasn't solely about fuckin'—it was about two souls laid bare. She made me want to do everything in my power to ensure I put every piece of her broken heart back together.

"What time is it?" Clover inquired, pulling my thoughts back to the moment.

"Shit, I don't know. Late."

"Do you think anything is open? All of a sudden, I'm starving."

"Good dick and company will do that to you," I joked.

She playfully rolled her eyes before grabbing her phone off the nightstand. "Whatever. It's almost eleven. I think I'm gonna try and order some pizza. I know a spot near the hospital that stays open until two in the morning."

"Call it in, and I'll pay for it."

"You're not one of those psychos that eat crazy shit on their pizza, are you?"

I chuckled. "Nah."

One side of her mouth lifted in a smile. "Good. I'm gonna go take a quick shower."

Clover tossed the sheets off and prepared to get up. The moment I saw her beautiful, bare curves, I reached out and reeled her back to me. "Let daddy make that pussy cum one more time."

"You're nasty, you know that?"

"I do."

A soft moan escaped her lips as I toyed with her nipples. "Mmm, shit. C'mon, Harlan. I wanna be out of the shower by the time the food gets here," she whined.

I kissed her neck as my hand found itself sandwiched between her warm thighs. "Mmm, you sure about that? To ignore that throbbing between your legs might be a recipe for disaster."

Clover smirked. "You're *so* bad for me."

"So?" I inquired before assailing her with a clever smile.

My phone rang just before I was about to slide back inside her. "Shit," I hissed, ready to ignore it.

The phone continued ringing insistently. Whoever was blowing me up wanted to make sure they gained my attention. An aggravated huff of air burst through my nostrils as I angrily swiped up my phone to see my aunt Wanda's name across the screen. My heart skipped a beat. She never called unless there was something wrong.

"H-hello?" I answered quickly.

"Harlan! I'm in the ambulance with your mother. She's being rushed to the hospital. I think she had a heart attack."

———

I rushed through the automatic sliding doors with Clover hot on my heels, shuffling by the waiting room full of worn chairs. I didn't stop until I was at the glassed-in reception area. "I need to see Marie Banks. She was transported here by ambulance."

"One moment," the receptionist stated before clicking away at the keyboard in front of her. "It looks like she's out of triage but is still being treated. Please have a seat in the waiting room, and I'll have the doctor come out and notify you when you can go back and see her," she explained.

"That's it? That's all you can tell me?" I asked.

"That's all the information I have right now, sir. Again, please have a seat, and the doctor will come out and speak with you."

We trekked back to the waiting room to sit with all the other worried family and friends crammed together. That was where I spotted my aunt Wanda keeping to herself in the corner. We traded glances before she shot up to her feet.

"Harlan!"

I shot toward her on unsteady legs and crashed into her with open arms. "Auntie, what happened? Have you heard anything? They not tellin' me shit up front!"

She shook her head. "I haven't gotten any updates since they took her back and started running tests."

"A heart attack? How did any of this happen?" I inquired, nerves completely shot to hell.

"She told me she was having chest pains that wouldn't go away. I asked her if she wanted me to come over and take her to the hospital.

Then she said, *Wanda, I think I'm having a heart attack.* My heart dropped. I told her to call nine-one-one immediately and that I was on my way. I pulled up at the same time as the paramedics, and they let me ride in the ambulance with her."

"Thank you for being there for her, Auntie."

"Of course. That's my sister. All we can do now is pray and wait for an update."

I took my seat beside her. "Auntie, this is Clover. Clover, this is my Aunt Wanda, my mother's baby sister."

Clover smiled. "Hi. It's nice to meet you."

Auntie quickly sized her up before returning a warm smile. "It's nice to meet you, too," she told her before trading silent glances with me. "Okay, nephew. I see you," she declared.

She knew I didn't bring anybody around my family, let alone the hospital to see my mother in the middle of an emergency. Clover was *that* special to me.

An hour passed, and the emergency room hadn't stopped buzzing with urgency—an eerie symphony of hushed conversations and hurried footsteps from doctors in white coats and people in different colored scrubs passing through the area without saying a damn thing to me. My heart pounded in sync with the chaos. I got antsy whenever someone passed by in a wheelchair or zoomed past on a stretcher. All I wanted was a fuckin' update on my mother.

"I'm about to go ask the receptionist what's going on back there," I announced.

Clover reached out to stop me before I lifted my body from the seat. "She doesn't know anything, Harlan. We just need to keep waiting for the doctor to come."

"I'm tired of waiting! Somebody needs to come out here and give me some fuckin' answers!" I hissed.

"Harlan, wait. When they know something, I'm sure they'll send someone out to update us. There's no sense in worrying everybody around here who have their own jobs to do."

A loud burst of air huffed through my nostrils as I ran my hand over the back of my head. "I just hate not knowing what the fuck is going on back there. Like, why the fuck haven't they come out and given an update?"

"Hospitals aren't run like fast-food restaurants, Harlan. If anything, they're probably running tests to find out what happened and then deciding what to do next to best treat her."

"I get it, but that don't mean I like that shit," I grumbled while stationing my eyes on the dusty artificial plant in the corner.

"Walk with me."

"Where?"

"I'm gonna hit up the coffee shop."

"Nah. I'll sit here in case they come while you're gone."

"Can I at least bring you back anything? They've got cookies, muffins, granola squares..."

"Nah. I'm straight. You go ahead."

"You sure? I could grab you a nasty cup of to-go coffee," she offered before cracking a slight smile.

"I'm sure."

"Would you like me to bring you back anything from the coffee shop?" Clover asked my aunt.

"No thank you, baby. But thank you for offering," she replied.

Just as Clover stood to leave, a fair-skinned doctor with half of his face hidden behind a surgical mask entered the waiting area. "Is the family of Marie Banks here?"

I shot to my feet. "I'm here!" I asserted while quickly approaching him. "I'm her son, Harlan, and this is her sister, Wanda. How is she?"

"Hi, Harlan. I'm Doctor Stokes, the head of cardiology here."

"How is she?" I repeated, not giving a fuck about his accolades at the moment.

He dropped his mask as grave lines etched into his forehead. "Your mother suffered a heart attack," he responded. "We're stabilizing her. She's in good hands."

"How did this happen?" Aunt Wanda interjected.

"We ran several tests, and one of them showed that she had a blocked artery. We did an emergency procedure called an angioplasty to unblock the blood vessel."

"Hold up. She had to have surgery?" I inquired.

"Yes. I inserted a small stent in her artery to keep it open and help keep the blood flowing to her heart."

I sighed. "Is she gonna be okay?"

"In short, yes. Your mom's lucky. If she hadn't gotten to the hospital when she did, her heart muscle would've started to deteriorate, which would have led to irreversible heart damage."

"Where is she now? Can we see her?" I asked.

"Yes. She's being transferred to the cardiology wing. Follow signs toward the elevator, then go up to the fourth floor. She's in room forty-one-seventeen."

"Thank you, Doctor," I acknowledged.

Aunt Wanda nodded, her voice a fragile whisper. "Thank you."

"You're very welcome," he replied before walking away.

"Are you coming up, Auntie?"

"You two go ahead. I'm gonna step outside and have a quick smoke then come up. He said room forty-one-seventeen, right?"

I bobbed my head. "Yeah."

"Okay."

———

"How are you feeling about all of this?" Clover probed as we stepped into the vacant elevator.

I jabbed the number four button before stepping back. "I don't know. All I know is I can't lose her. I've already lost too much. Outside of my boys and my auntie, she's the only family I have left."

Clover reached out to squeeze my hand. "This might not mean much right now, but you've got me."

"That means everything right now," I assured her before pulling her into a warm embrace.

Her eyes held a calm resolve. "I know this is scary, but the good news is she survived."

I agreed with a nod. Little did she know I wasn't scared. I was angry. "That is good news."

I swept her hand in mine as we stepped off the elevator. We drifted down the long, maze-like hallways toward the cardiology wing. As we trekked under the bright lighting, the bare walls were covered in muted paint. I was grateful my mother survived her heart attack. More than anything, I appreciated how willing Clover was to drop everything and come with me. She'd insisted on coming, even though I protested. But as I continued to assess the situation, I couldn't help but realize how right she was. Having her by my side meant more to me than she knew.

"You ready to go see her?" Clover asked as we approached my mother's hospital room.

My chest deflated with a hard sigh. "Yeah."

"Do you want me to give you a minute alone?"

I tilted my head to the left. "Nah. You not leavin' my side, Lady Luck. I need you."

"Then you got me," she replied.

I pushed open the door and raced to my mother's bedside. I clutched her hand as she lay on the sterile bed. There was an oxygen mask over her mahogany face. The heart monitor beeped—a rhythm of hope easing my nerves with each beat. Clover stood behind me, resting a supportive hand on my shoulder to let me know she wasn't far away.

I leaned forward to kiss my mother's forehead. "I'm right here, Mama, and Aunt Wanda is on her way up, too," I whispered to her.

Aunt Wanda entered the room fifteen minutes later. She stopped by the hand sanitizing station at the front of the room before proceeding inside. The next few hours stretched on as the three of us remained by my mama's side. Auntie and Clover took turns adjusting her pillows, whispering soothing words, and praying over her as she slept. I watched her chest rise and fall, never missing a beat until her eyes slowly fluttered open.

My heart leapt out of my chest. "Mama."

"Harlan," she murmured after slowly pulling down the oxygen mask. She looked at me and my auntie before her weary eyes landed on Clover's. "Who's this?"

I squeezed her hand. "Mama, this is Clover. She's a nurse, and more importantly, she's my girl," I declared, putting the official stamp on our relationship.

A smile spread across Clover's face as she leaned forward and touched her hand gently. "It's so nice to meet you. You're going to be okay. We're here for you."

My mother studied Clover in the same manner my auntie had. Her gaze was sharp despite whatever pain she was in. "Harlan," she whispered, "are you trying to make me have another heart attack? She's gorgeous."

"Yeah. She is a beauty," I agreed with a smirk.

Clover smiled before moving about the room. I twisted my neck to see her standing by the whiteboard with my mother's information, the name of the nurse on call, her medications, diet restrictions, and scheduled tests. She looked as if she was studying it. There was a knock on the door before I could quiz her on what she was doing. Doctor Stokes stepped inside soon after, and Clover immediately stepped forward.

"Doctor," she acknowledged, "I saw on the board that she's on beta-blockers for hypertension. Are you ensuring you're titrating them appropriately to prevent further strain on her heart?"

The doctor raised an eyebrow, impressed. "You're a nurse?"

She dipped her chin in a confident nod. "Yes, and I'm also her son's girlfriend."

I watched in awe as Clover advocated for my mother as if she were her own—her voice steady, her knowledge evident. She wasn't just a nurse; she was as fierce of a protector as I was. My admiration for her swelled in my chest as my mother squeezed my hand. She mouthed the words *she's a keeper* before lifting her lips in a slight smile. I blinked, partially stunned. Having my mother's approval meant more than I'd admit. But it wasn't just that. It was the way Clover cared—for my mother, for me. She'd stepped into my chaos with unwavering compassion and held me down when I faltered. Before Clover, I never wanted to know what it felt like to fall in love. But I couldn't help myself around her. In that sterile room, I realized I'd fallen in love with her— not just for her beauty, but for her pure heart. She'd become a part of my hectic story, woven into the fabric of my fast and furious life. I couldn't stop my mother's words from echoing in my head: *She's a keeper.* I was ready to give her my heart and my last name.

"Thank you for being here, baby, and for introducing me to Clover."

"It was so good to meet you," Clover told her. "I'm sure we'll meet again. For now, get your rest."

"I second that," Aunt Wanda chimed in.

When my mother finally drifted back off to sleep, my aunt swept a stray hair from her forehead. "Go ahead and go home, Harlan. She'll be okay. My big sis is strong. We'll get her through this," she commented softly but assuredly.

My heart was a tangle of gratitude and uncertainty. I knew she was in good hands, but I still didn't want to leave her side. I shifted to Clover. "How do you do this shit every day?"

Clover smiled, her eyes reflecting the fluorescent glow of the lights overhead. "Because every patient is someone's mother, sister, daughter, or aunt. And, sometimes, love is the best medicine."

"Amen to that," Aunt Wanda chimed in with a church wave.

"Do you wanna go?" I asked Clover.

She uncurled her body from the chair in the corner and stretched. "I wanna do whatever you wanna do. I'm here to support you," she confirmed, voice oozing with love and care.

As if my feelings hadn't been stamped, her response told me everything I felt was true. Clover was more than a keeper; she was my lifeline.

CLOVER

One week later.

The sunlight streamed through the salon window, casting warm hues on my freshly painted toes. I wiggled them, savoring the softness of the pedicure. My mother, Evelyn, sat beside me, leaning back in the massage chair with her eyes closed. Since we'd made things official, I'd been trying to find the right time to tell her about Harlan and me. I hadn't brought a man around my parents in a long time. Their expectations were exceedingly high. Plus, it didn't help that they were still emotionally attached to Lorenzo as if he were still walking the earth.

"Mom," I began, "I've been seeing someone."

Her eyes snapped open, curiosity dancing in her pools of brown. "*Really*? What's his name? What's he do? Where'd you meet? Tell me everything!" she insisted.

I hesitated for a second then took a deep breath. "His name is Harlan," I replied. "We met at a bar when I was out with some friends. He's a mechanic—passionate about motorcycles and engines, just like Dad was into antique cars way back in the day."

Her crooked smile wavered. "And you think you're ready?"

I studied my French tip-painted toenails. "I've never felt more ready,

Mom. It's been two years since Zo passed. Harlan makes me laugh. He makes me feel safe, and healing isn't a straight line from broken to better, but he's helped fill this gaping hole in my heart I never thought would be whole again."

My mother reached for my hand. "Your heart is resilient," she acknowledged. "And I know Lorenzo would want you to find joy again."

I nodded. "I'd like to think so, too."

"You know we're having our annual spring barbecue this weekend," she reminded me. "You should bring him."

My eyes widened. "Mom, no. We—"

She raised a questioning brow. "Clover Alexandria Baldwin, I'm *not* taking no for an answer! Bring Harlan. Let us meet him properly."

I sighed. If there was one thing Evelyn Baldwin hated, it was being told no. Fighting her on the matter would only tire me out. Besides, as much as Harlan had my legs open like a 7-Eleven at midnight, it was only fitting that he met the two most important people to me. "Fine. We'll be there."

———

And so, Saturday finally rolled around. Harlan sat strapped in my passenger seat as I drove through the wrought-iron gates of my parent's estate, leading up the long driveway. I'd been so on edge about introducing him to my parents for the first time that I hadn't had time to process the offer letter I'd received the day prior for my first travel nurse assignment in New York. Deep down, I was excited about the new opportunity but didn't know how to tell my family or Harlan about it.

Harlan's brown eyes popped wide as he soaked it all in. "Damn. Your childhood home is like a goddamn fairytale or somethin'," he mumbled as he looked out the window.

The Baldwin Estate, my childhood home, stood firm, looking as pristine as it did when I ran through the long, empty halls as a kid. The manicured lawns seemed to stretch to infinity. The mansion's beauty was matched only by the wealth that had birthed it—a lineage of unapologetic Black privilege. My parents, Evelyn and James Baldwin, were the definition of a power couple. They both graduated summa cum laude from Howard University in the eighties. My father went on to become a plastic surgeon, while my mother became a psychiatrist who eventually opened up her own practice. They worked hard for every promotion as they made their way up, bursting through the glass ceilings in their fields. I grew up in the realm of Jack and Jill playdates and cotillions, whereas Harlan had made it clear he'd grown up in a different world—one of grease-streaked overalls, oil-scented garages, and the roar of motorcycle engines.

"You sure you're ready for this?" I asked him as I parked the car and shut off the engine.

"As ready as I'll ever be."

"You ever met a girl's parents before?"

Harlan cast a smile at me. "Nah. I ain't never worn no tie either," he replied before flipping down the visor to adjust it around his neck.

I admired how handsome he looked in his suit, no matter how uncomfortable he felt. Our family barbecues weren't like everyone else's. Ours were a parade of prosperity—complete with the clink of crystal glasses, the murmur of silk-clad guests, and the scent of fresh, chilled shrimp mingling with the fresh jasmine blooms my mother had planted each spring.

"You look good, better than good, actually," I complimented him before leaning over the center console to kiss his cheek. "Now, let's go. I'm sure Mom and Dad will be happy to see us."

We stepped out of the car and went through the house to the backyard to find my parents on the veranda. My father sat nursing a glass of bourbon in his hand with his *Kiss the Chef* apron laid across the table for show. I hadn't seen him flip a burger on the grill since I was a kid. Still, my heart swelled from the nostalgia. In the background, hired waiters, dressed in black and white, moved with silent precision. Their shoes barely whispered against the marble tiles as they set up tables covered in steamed white linen. The silverware gleamed, and crystal glasses sparkled in the sunlight. Each place setting was perfect—a delicate porcelain plate, a silver fork, and a monogrammed "B" napkin folded into a perfect triangle.

My mother stood, smoothing her hands down the front of her dress. "Clover, you're here."

The backyard bloomed with the scent of lobster bisque and macaroons as I leaned into my mother's embrace. "Hey, Mom."

My father's eyes crinkled when he smiled. "Hey, princess!"

"Mom... Dad... I'd like for you to meet my boyfriend, Harlan."

My mother sipped her lemonade before speaking. "I'm Clover's mother, Evelyn. It's nice to meet you."

Harlan extended his hand. "Likewise, Mrs. Baldwin. I can see where Clover gets her beauty from."

My mother's smile was as polished as her silverware. "Thank you."

"It's good to meet you too, Mr. Baldwin."

Harlan and my father exchanged a firm handshake. "Welcome to our home, Harlan. Glad you could make it."

"It's dope. I mean, *nice*. You have a nice home," Harlan corrected, polishing his grammar.

After introductions, I watched my parents assess Harlan with intense scrutiny in their eyes. I could feel them nitpicking everything they considered to be flaws. My mother's smile turned frosty as her gaze lingered on the tattoos on Harlan's hands.

I nervously looked around to see there were no other guests around aside from the head waiter standing near the veranda railing. "Where's everybody else?"

"On the way. We wanted you two to arrive earlier so we'd have time to speak with Harlan privately."

"Let's sit, shall we?" my father insisted before folding his body into one of the patio chairs. "So, Harlan, what do you do?"

Harlan squared his shoulders as he took his seat across from my father. "I run an auto repair shop," he replied proudly. "It was my father's, and I'm carrying on the legacy."

My mother's microbladed eyebrow arched. "No college degree?"

Harlan's eyes met mine before he cleared his throat. "No, ma'am. I believe in learning by doing," he answered her. "My father built something from scratch—the shop, the community it serves. Entrepreneurship is my degree."

My father's lips tightened. "I'll admit college isn't for everyone. Tell us about where you grew up. Where'd you graduate high school?"

"I grew up in a low-income neighborhood on the south side of Chicago. I went to mediocre public schools all my life, where my brother and I got free lunch. My parents couldn't afford to send us to private school. Is there anything else you'd like to know?" he snapped.

My father scoffed. "An inner-city hoodlum. How original."

"Dad!" I hissed as my brows dipped low in disapproval.

Harlan's brow creased. "What's that supposed to mean?"

My mother interjected. "I think what he's trying to say is, what can you offer our daughter?"

Harlan's gaze shifted to mine. "Respect. Partnership. Protection. Love."

My parents were unmoved by his response. "Don't you think our daughter deserved more? Someone with credentials, at the least, some connections? Because I sure do," my mother spat.

I was mortified. My voice trembled as I spoke. "Mom, Dad, Harlan is perfect for me. He's loyal and hardworking, and he cares about me. Most importantly, he makes me happy. That's *all* you should want for me."

My mother leaned over and squeezed my shoulder as the first set of guests began to arrive, their footsteps echoing in the background. "Of course we want you to be happy, sweetheart, but why can't you do that with someone more on your level? I mean, you expect us to give our blessings to *this*...?"

"Your mother's got a point, princess. Lorenzo fit seamlessly into our family tapestry, but this one, I'm not so sure," my father retorted as he wagged his head in disapproval.

"With all due respect, sir, I didn't think I was going to get your fuckin' blessing, even if I *did* want that shit. You and your wife had your minds made up about me the moment you saw me. But I am who the fuck I am, whether you like it or not! And guess what? That shit ain't about to change," Harlan retorted.

My heart sank as tears blurred my vision. He shouldn't have had to defend himself to my parents like that. I shot up to my feet, unable to stomach any more of the toxic back and forth. I'd never been more uncomfortable hearing Lorenzo's name being brought up in a conversation.

"Everyone, stop it! Just stop it! I can't believe what I'm hearing right now! I can see it was a mistake bringing Harlan here and exposing him to this disgusting behavior! You could've at least tried to get to know him before you judged him! But if you can't accept him, you can't accept me. We're leaving!" I announced without a second thought.

And with that, I stormed out—the echo of my footsteps shattering my parents' facade of the *perfect* Black family. Harlan followed suit, leaving them at the table in stunned silence. All my hopes of my parents chatting and laughing with Harlan while making a real effort to get to know him had crashed and burned within fifteen minutes. Clearly, all they cared about was a lineage as pristine as their porcelain plates.

Outside, I leaned against the stone wall, breath ragged as my chest heaved with rage. I didn't know if I was madder or more hurt. Harlan found me and extended his arms, giving me the embrace we both knew I desperately needed.

"Harlan, I'm so sorry. If I knew they were gonna grill you and act like that, I would've never—"

He cut me off. "Nah. It's cool."

"No. That shit isn't cool at all. Fuck them for acting like that! Seriously! I don't care what they think or what they say. You help me come alive. With you, I don't feel like I'm drowning anymore. You're the one I choose, Harlan. I want you. I... I *love* you," I confessed as tears streamed down my cheeks.

"I love you, too," he replied before I felt his warm lips mash against my forehead.

I didn't give a damn what my parents or anyone else had to say. For me, Harlan was more than perfect—he was everything to me.

———

The sun dipped below the horizon as Harlan and I approached my apartment. The only good thing that I could say came out of the day was our exchange of the three most important words anyone could say to someone. I was proud to be loved by Harlan and even prouder to love him back. He was the first man I'd unlocked my heart for since losing Lorenzo, and I felt it was only right to tell him the entire backstory of the rise and fall of my previous relationship.

I turned to him after shutting the engine off. "Are you still upset about today?"

"Nah. I've been called a lot worse from better mothafuckas. It'll take a lot more than that to get under my skin. What about you? You good?"

A wrinkle cut across my brow. "Far from it. I still can't believe they talked to you like that. I'm glad you held your own, but I'm sorry you even had to do that. I don't know. I felt like I took you to the lion's den and left you to be devoured," I confessed.

"You must not have seen the way your parents were lookin' when you popped off on their asses behind me, but I sure did. You ain't leave me to fight shit alone. I'm always gon' hold my own, but you had my back out there. I respect it."

"I'm glad you feel that way, especially with my father bringing up my ex. I swear I've never been more embarrassed in my life."

"I'm sorry they did that shit to you," he acknowledged before reaching out to place his hand on my thigh.

I huffed. "Yeah, me too. But speaking of my ex, I know I've only told you bits and pieces about my past, but now that we've taken our relationship to the next level, I'm ready to share everything with you," I announced. "All the dark, gritty parts of it. But only if you want to know."

"I wanna know everything about you, Lady Luck, good or bad."

A slow smile crawled up one side of my face before I turned my gaze to the other parked cars around us in the lot. "We met in some nameless antique shop tucked away from all the madness in the city. I stepped inside to better see the celestial artifacts I'd been drawn to in the store window. It only got better inside. There were vintage telescopes, constellation maps, and a brass astrolabe," I blabbed.

Harlan chuckled. "A what?"

"Sorry. Think of it like a brass compass. It can function as a rotating celestial map and be used for navigation, hence the compass comment. But, anyway, Zo was already there. When our eyes met, it was as if the entire universe paused. He smiled. I smiled back. As much smiling as I was doing, I could barely catch my breath. He approached me. We talked about the stars. Because what else would two Black twenty-somethings nerding out in antique shops talk about, right? It was the first thing we bonded on."

"Sounds like your parents loved 'em."

"They did. We were sophomores in college, both young and passionate. He bonded with my father over his love for golfing. Zo worked at a country club, so he got good at it. He and my dad would travel to tournaments and everything."

"Damn."

"Yeah. It was a different time."

"So, your ex came from money?"

"Yes and no. He used his uncle's address to attend school in a different zone and worked at the country club. He looked the part more than anything."

"How long did y'all date?"

"Four years before he proposed. We'd only been engaged for six months before he... the morning he died, we were coming out of our favorite coffee shop downtown when he collapsed in the middle of the street. My entire world blurred. All I remember is the wailing of the sirens as I squeezed his hand in the back of the ambulance all the way to the hospital. When we got there, his pulse had become thready. The doctors discovered an undiagnosed brain aneurysm—a literal ticking time bomb in his head. They rushed him into surgery, but there was an unexpected bleed. Just like that, he was stolen from me before I had the chance to say goodbye."

Harlan lowered his head out of respect. "I'm sorry for your loss, for real. I know that had to be tough."

"Tough is an understatement. It was excruciating."

"Trust me, I can relate."

I drew in a deep breath. "There's something else I need to tell you."

"About your ex?"

"No," I answered. I'd rehearsed the words a few hundred times on the drive from my parents, but when the moment presented itself, I felt my courage waver. "I, uh, interviewed for a traveling nurse position a couple of weeks ago and got an email with the offer letter yesterday."

His brows furrowed. "Congratulations! But what does your job offer mean for us?"

My fingers twisted nervously in my lap. "It means I'll be moving," I admitted. "To different cities, different hospitals. It's a chance to explore the country, to make a real difference."

"And us?"

My gaze met his. "I want you to consider coming with me."

"Coming with you where?"

"Well, to New York, for starters."

Harlan's eyes ballooned before going back to their normal size. "You want me to leave Chicago?"

I nodded. "Yeah. Leave Chicago. Be with me."

Harlan blinked. "But we've only been together for—"

"I know," I interjected. "But I don't think how we feel about each other should be measured in the time we've been together. All I know is I don't want to lose what I have with you."

His jaw tightened. "What about my shop? My family? My riders?"

I leaned in closer. "I don't have all the answers. But I do know that families visit, and there's always FaceTime calls between holidays. But this—this is *our* chance to write our love story how we want to, Harlan."

He sighed, apprehension apparent in his body language. "What if it doesn't work out? Are you ready for me to burn down the world behind you, Lady Luck?"

"But what if it does? Don't you wanna discover new cities and fall even deeper in love with me?"

He studied the hope in my eyes before speaking. "This ain't a movie. This is real life you're talking about. You know I'm new to this love shit. What if I get to New York and realize I'm not ready? I don't wanna break your heart."

"Then don't," I responded, taking his hand in mine. "Sometimes love means taking an unexpected leap of faith."

Harlan traced slow circles into my palm before reeling me into his arms. "I can't believe you're asking me to leave everything I love behind, and I'm actually fuckin' considering that shit," he acknowledged.

"At least I'm asking you to leave everything for something great— our future."

His lips brushed against my forehead. "I swear I better not regret this shit."

I smiled. "So, is that a yes?"

"It's a yes," Harlan agreed.

I squealed before tossing my arms around his neck. And so, in the intimate quiet of my car, we decided to take a leap fueled by our newfound love. Within a few weeks, Chicago would become a distant memory, and the entire country would be our blank canvas.

HARLAN

A few days later, my knuckles collided with my mother's front door before I took a few steps back and waited for her to answer. She welcomed me inside with the familiar, warm smile I'd been used to seeing all my life. The air smelled like coffee and comforting memories. I couldn't have been more grateful that she'd survived the heart attack and was back home resting. I entered the cozy living room, where filtered sun rays peeked through her lace curtains. She sat in my father's favorite armchair, which, over the years, had become hers. My eyes caught the framed family photos on the mantelpiece. My best childhood memories were frozen in time. Had it not been for Clover walking into my life, I would've sworn my best days were behind me. But I had something to look forward to with her by my side.

I looked at her with concern etched into my expression. "How you feelin' today, Mama?" I quizzed. "And be straight up with me."

"I'm okay, Harlan. Your aunt Wanda ain't been too long left from here, making sure I took all my medications and whatnot. You know how worrisome my sister can be," she commented, followed by a soft chuckle.

"Good. I'm glad you got somebody stayin' on top of you with your meds and everything. That makes what I'm about to say a little easier."

"I knew something else besides your mother's health was on your mind. C'mon and spill it. Tell me what's on your mind."

I took a deep breath. "Well, you know your heart attack had scared the hell out of me. Made me start rethinking a lot of shit. I mean, things."

"You're my heart, and I know seeing me go through that... it was hard on you, especially after losing your father like that when you were younger," she said softly. "But lucky for you, your mama is a fighter."

"I've been thinking about life, Mama, about what truly matters to me and what I want my future to look like. And... I've made a decision."

"I'm listening."

"I'm leaving Chicago. Clover got a new job in New York, and I'm going with her."

Her brows rose with surprise. "New York? But what about the auto repair shop? Our family has poured our blood, sweat, and tears into it for years. You know I'm too sick to run it full-time like I used to."

"I know, Mama. I'd never ask you to do that. The shop means everything to me, but Clover's New York job opportunity is a game-changer for her. And well, she's my game-changer."

A proud grin exposed her teeth. "Ah, Clover. I may have been pumped up on medication at the time, but I saw the way she looks at you in that hospital room, Harlan. That girl adores you. I think she's good for you. Your aunt Wanda thinks so, too. She brings out the best in you."

"Y'all was in here talkin' about me?"

"Yeah. So? I can't talk about my son and his new love?"

I huffed. "I'm glad y'all like her. I wish I could say the same was true for her parents. They took one look at me and hated my ass."

"Why?"

Doubt pinched my forehead in the middle. "Hell if I know. I wore a suit and tie, lookin' casket sharp. We didn't stay past twenty minutes."

"If this is the girl you wanna be with for the long haul, you're going to have to find a way to get along with her family, Harlan."

"Not if we're in New York," I replied with a soft chuckle.

"You're a trip, boy. Remember: you can't cut corners when it comes to love or family ties," she advised.

"But leaving the shop, our family's legacy in someone else's hands... I don't know. I told her I'd go, but I'm still torn."

The shop was my safe haven of grease-stained overalls and the purr of engines. Leaving it behind would be like leaving a piece of myself behind too.

"You didn't sound torn when you sat here and told me you were moving to New York, Harlan. You didn't say, *Mama, I think I'm going.* You said, *I'm leaving Chicago.* Your mind is already made up, Harlan. Your mind and your heart. The only thing to do now is figure out what to do with the shop."

Her comment had brought me back to the thoughts I'd been wrestling with all night. Who would I hand over the business to? What would happen with The Spades? Most importantly, how would I feel if I left the city without finding out who killed my brother?

"Listen to me, Harlan, and hear me good. Life isn't just about engines and oil stains. It's about love, passion, and, most importantly, following *your* heart. Your father and I built that shop so you and your brother could have choices. So you could chase your dreams. And if Clover is your dream, then you gotta go."

"I just don't wanna disappoint you."

"You won't. If anything, I'd be disappointed if you didn't take the chance. You have my blessing, Harlan. Besides, I already told you Clover's a keeper. I adore her."

I smiled without showing my teeth. "Thanks, Mama. I needed to hear that."

"Oh, I know. Mama always knows." She winked. "When do you leave?"

I shrugged. "I'm not sure yet. She just told me about the job offer yesterday. We haven't worked out all of the details."

"Well, be sure to bring her by before you go for a proper visit now that I'm out of the hospital."

"For sure," I agreed with a quick nod before standing up to hug her.

———

Later that morning, I was working on a custom paint job at the shop when Chop walked into the garage with his dreads pulled back into a ponytail. I lifted the clear protective glasses from over my eyes and rested them on my head. I pulled off my gloves before dapping him up.

"'Sup, Chop?" I greeted him.

"'Sup, nigga? Workin' your magic, I see."

"Wanted to do something dope for Zyon after his bike got fucked up after he won the race at the meet. A couple more coats and it'll be finished."

He pulled up a crate and sat on it. "Shit looks fire," he complimented, eyeing the fresh coat of black paint and red flames on the side.

"Thanks."

"So, wassup? You hit my line early as hell this morning. What you wanna rap about so damn bad?"

I huffed before drawing my eyes up to his. "I'm leaving Chicago, man."

His brows heightened toward his crisp hairline. "Leaving? Nigga, fuck you mean leaving? Like, for a vacation or somethin' more permanent?"

"More permanent. I've been keepin' shit under wraps for a little while now, but you remember the girl I told you I met? The one who backed into my car that night at the club?"

"Yeah. What about her?"

"She's my girl, and we're moving to New York," I stated, dropping two bombs on him at once.

"New York? That's a leap. No disrespect, but how long you been layin' down with this broad, Harlan?"

"Not long. But it feels like a lifetime. She's... different, my nigga. I ain't ever met another like her."

Chop raised an eyebrow. "Different how? Sounds like she got you drinkin' the Kool-Aid early, my boy."

"I don't know how to explain it. She's got this fire in her, Chop. Plus, she's a damn good nurse. You should've seen her when Mama had her heart attack. I don't know what I did to deserve her, but I swear her ass was heaven-sent."

"Look, nigga. You a grown-ass man. Plus, I can hear it in your voice that you care about her. But to uproot your life for her? Nah, yo. That ain't like you. That ain't the Harlan I know."

"She got me thinking different and feeling different, too," I admitted.

"I can tell. But since you haven't introduced us, what's she like?"

"Clover? Shit, yo. She's got these beautiful eyes—like she's seen both heaven and hell. And she's smart and gentle. She's got this laugh that lights up a room."

"Sounds like she's got your nose wide open. But, still, leaving the shop? Your mom? What about The Spades? What about Low's murder? Don't you still want justice for him?"

A long sigh escaped my nostrils. "Of course, I want justice for my brother, nigga. Me leaving doesn't change that shit."

"Then what's the rush to move to New York when we still got unfinished business here? Why not let her go and visit when you can?"

"Because I fuckin' love her, nigga," I confessed.

Chop and I were boys, but we ain't share feelings regularly. We shed tears together when Low died, but I hadn't talked about matters of the heart since.

He sucked his teeth. "Damn, nigga. You got it bad, bad."

I huffed. "I know. I'm still working out the kinks with everything, but I'm thinkin' about flying back and forth for the first few months. And as far as Mama, she's tough. Plus, she's got my aunt Wanda. And you, Chop. I need you to check in on her from time to time and watch over my guys here at the shop."

"Me?"

"Who else? With Low gone, you're the closest thing I got to family. Me and you go back beyond The Spades."

If I were being honest with him and myself, I would've said I'd grown tired of the motorcycle club life ever since Low died. But I didn't. I ain't wanna put no more pressure on him than I already had. I'd been trying to get Chop to move up since Low's passing, but he wasn't hearing it. I couldn't blame him. He liked his role, and he played it well.

"I can tell you're burnt out. Maybe a change of scenery would be good for you," Chop announced without me having to say shit.

I turned away as a smirk stretched up one side of my mouth. That was why he was my nigga. Aside from my brother, Chop was the closest man living to me. I didn't take that shit lightly. His opinion mattered to me. It just didn't matter more to me than my own. Before I could respond, I looked up to see Clover walking in carrying a plastic takeout bag. Her yellow and white tie-dye sundress had a deep neck plunge and a split up the left side that exposed her juicy thigh with each step she took. She smiled when her eyes met mine. I waved her over.

"Hey, baby. Surprise!"

I grinned. "Whatchu doin' here, Lady Luck?"

"It was my day off, so I thought I'd surprise you with lunch. And... *maybe* see if you could look at my friend's truck. Do you remember our little taillight mishap from a few weeks back? Well, she got her cousin to fix it quickly, and it's a mess. So, I figured I'd kill two birds with one stone and bring it by while she's at work. It's the least I can do before we —" she stopped talking when she noticed Chop sitting off to the side. "Oh! I'm sorry. I didn't know you had company. Hi!"

"Yo, Chop. This is my girl, Clover. Clover, this is my boy, Chop."

Clover extended her hand to him. "Nice to meet you. Harlan has told me a story or two."

"You got my nigga pillow talkin' and tellin' stories, huh? Well, buckle up, Clover. You're in for a wild ride."

"Thanks for lunch. I'll come out and take a look at that taillight."

"Well, look, I'll let you get to that. We'll finish up our conversation later, aight? I'm out," Chop announced before dapping me up.

"You sure?"

"Yeah. I'll hit you later."

———

Once Chop left, I fixed the taillight on Clover's friend's ride before heading back inside to have lunch with Clover. It was the first time she'd come to the shop. And as happy as I was to see her, I wasn't big on surprises. My discontent faded when the grilled cheese and tomato soup aroma wafted past my nose as Clover unpacked the lunch in my office.

Clover grinned. "I hope you're hungry."

"For sure, but what's the occasion?"

"Well, I do have a pretty big update," she teased mid-chew.

"'Sup?"

She clasped her hands together. "I officially accepted the job offer in New York. The hospital's giving me three weeks to relocate."

I froze. "*Three* weeks? That's... fast."

Her eyes searched my face for a positive reaction, but I didn't have one to give her. She sighed. "I know. You're not having second thoughts about coming with me, right?"

"Clover, I've still got a lot of loose ends to tie up here. I've got the shop, my mom—"

She placed her soft hand on mine. "Harlan, it's okay. We'll figure it out. You can tie up loose ends here while I set things up in New York."

"Traveling back and forth?"

She nodded before sweeping her hand against my cheek. "Exactly. For however long, we'll make it work. Whatever we have to do to be together. I'm happy you're making this leap with me, baby."

I smiled before turning my lips to kiss her palm. "I love you, Clover."

"I love you too," she replied before sealing her lips against mine. "Since it's my first time here, I think it's only right that you give me a tour of the shop."

The familiar scent of motor oil enveloped us as we entered the garage. "Welcome to my playhouse and my safe haven," I announced with a grin as I laced her fingers with mine.

I led her past rows of tool-laden workbenches as the air hummed. "It's gritty. I love it."

"Over there, we've got the engine bay. And this corner? That's where we resurrect old classics," I explained as we approached a sleek motorcycle with its custom paint gleaming under the fluorescent lights. "This is what I'm working on right now."

Her brows raised toward her hairline as she eyed my half-finished masterpiece. "Wow. What a beauty. You're truly talented, Harlan," she complimented me.

"From one beauty to another," I said as I walked up behind her and slipped my arms around her waist.

"You're welcome, baby."

I peppered light kisses against the side of her neck while my hands roamed over her curves. "Thank you again for lunch, but now I'm ready for dessert."

CLOVER

Harlan's soft yet barbaric growl in my ear made me clench my thighs. He spun me around to face him and pressed my body against his hard chest. "Here?" I whispered before attempting to look over my shoulder.

Harlan hooked his finger underneath my chin and slowly twisted my neck back toward him. "Right here. Right now," he answered.

"We gotta be quick. Q is gonna want her car back before she gets off," I reminded him with a seductive smirk.

"Say less."

"Oooh!" I squealed as he lifted me into his arms and set me on the hood of Quintessa's car.

His kissable lips latched onto mine. I hooked my arms around his neck and pulled him closer, savoring each second of our kiss.

"You ever heard of soul ties?" Harlan inquired as he gently bit my lip.

I quickly lifted his oil-stained wife beater over his head while nodding. "Mmhm," I answered as my fingertips skated up and down his exposed, muscular biceps.

"It's gotta be the only thing to explain our connection, right?"

"Abso-fuckin-lutely."

Harlan didn't even bother to take off my dress. He just pulled it up over my waist and slid my panties down over my knees. I licked my palm before sliding it between my legs to ensure I was nice and wet for him. He grasped my knees and eased them apart. He forcefully pushed my legs up to my chest and peppered kisses against the back of my soft thighs.

"Mmm, fine and flexible. A deadly combination," Harlan growled.

Passionate moans slipped past my lips as he latched his lips onto my clit and sucked it hungrily.

I gasped as my eyes rolled to the back of my head. "Ooooh shit. Yessss."

Harlan pinned my legs back to finger my love box while burying his face between my sticky, wet thighs. After lapping my pussy like a kitten to warm milk, he peeled my body off the hood and bent me over it. He finger fucked me from behind while unzipping his pants. I looked over my shoulder to see his erection standing at full attention. The second he slid inside me, his dick had me singing.

"Oooh shit!" I squealed, pulling myself up on the tips of my toes as I absorbed the sweet feeling of him deep inside me.

Harlan's calloused hands gripped my hips, dipping deeper. "That pussy stays wet for me," he roared while smacking my ass.

I bucked back against him like a wild, raging bull. "Yes, baby! You feel so good!"

My loud, carefree moans filled the garage as Harlan pumped quickly. He gripped a handful of my hair, yanked it back with one hand, and cupped my throat with his other.

"Take every inch of this dick. It's all for you, Lady Luck," he promised.

Somehow, I found myself on my back on top of the hood. Harlan's wild and fierce possession of my body had me in a trance. My legs dangled in the air as we watched his dick snake in and out of me. His dick came out creamier and creamier with every stroke.

"Ooh fuck. Look what that pretty pussy did," Harlan grunted while tapping his thick dick against my clit.

His hand firmly gripped my breast, thumbing my nipple as my legs hung over his shoulders. I tossed my head back and moaned as he pushed back inside and drilled into me. "Mmmm, shit."

"Mmhmm. I know this that shit that you like."

I moaned while locking eyes with him. "I love it, baby. Keep doing it just like that."

"You're all fuckin' mine, Clover. I love you. Don't you ever forget that shit," he growled while grabbing my throat.

Harlan never broke eye contact with me. I thought I'd melt in a puddle of lust and emotion. "Yes! I'm yours, baby! I promise," I panted. "I love you, too."

The feeling of Harlan inside me felt too good to stop. I hooked my legs around his waist to keep the slick heat of his body tightly pinned against mine.

"You tryna make a nigga splatter cum all over your walls, ain't you? Is that what you want? You want daddy to cum inside you?" Harlan snarled in my ear.

"Yes, baby! Don't stop fuckin' me!" I squealed, taking each deep stroke until he came.

———

The next day, I headed to a pharmacy to grab a Plan B before my shift started after Harlan beat my pussy like Holyfield in his shop. New York was right around the corner, and I couldn't afford any mishaps. *Three weeks until New York. I can do this.* When my phone buzzed, I pulled into a parking spot underneath the pharmacy's flickering fluorescent lights. The caller ID read Travel Nurse Agency, and my heart skipped a beat.

"Hello?" I answered.

"Clover, hi. It's Maegan, the HR manager here in New York. I'm just calling to say that everything on our end for your housing and start date is confirmed. You'll start on the fifteenth of next month. Does that work for you?"

"Yes, thank you. I'm in."

"Great. We'll see you on the fifteenth," she replied before ending the call.

I tossed my phone in my purse before opening the driver's side door to get out. I trekked down the sidewalk before hearing a familiar voice call out to me before I could step into the bustling pharmacy.

"What's good, sis?"

I snapped my neck to see Lux standing a few paces behind me, puffing a cigarette. "Lux? Long time no see. What are you doing *here* of all places?" I quizzed, aiming my index finger at the pharmacy.

He tipped his head toward the brick-and-mortar establishment. "Got a lil pharmacy broad on the inside that do whatever I say when I say. I'm waitin' for her ass to come out now with some work. What about chu?"

My mind raced as I quickly thought of a lie. "Me? Oh, I'm just running some errands on my lunch break. They're always running good deals on water and snacks here."

His eyes were guarded as he nodded. "Mmm. So, what's new?"

My heart raced. I couldn't reveal my plans to him. "Oh, you know. Work. Life."

My eyes drifted to his exposed tricep, where the inked snake emblem of the Diablo Disciple motorcycle club was etched into his honey-brown skin. A lightbulb went off. They were rivals of Harlan's club, and I didn't want my past ties to intertwine with my future. Part of me still loved Lux like a brother, but the less time I spent around him the better.

My eyes popped wide as I stammered nervously. "Lux, listen, I—"

"Yeah?" he asked, leaning against the wall before taking another puff.

I glanced around, spotting the pharmacy entrance and my parked car. There was no way I would enter the pharmacy to get what I'd come for with Lorenzo's brother breathing down my neck. I pulled my phone out of my purse and pretended to look alarmed. "Hey, I've got to go. There's an emergency at the hospital. See you around."

"Bet. Take care, sis."

I hurried back to my car and got inside, heart pounding. After the door closed and locked behind me, I blew out a breath I didn't even know I was holding. As I pulled off, I realized some secrets were best kept in the shadows.

———

The familiar fluorescent lights shone over the bustling ER as I smoothed out the slight wrinkles in my light blue scrubs. I was still rattled after my random run-in with Lux and had lost my appetite because of it. I chugged down the last bit of my smoothie, hoping to sneak off to the cafeteria for some real sustenance later.

As the minutes on the clock inched by, I found myself caught up in paperwork and moving from one bed to another, tending to patients. My stomach grumbled in protest all the way. Suddenly, the automatic ER doors parted as Harlan swaggered in, holding the handles of a brown paper bag. His eyes locked on mine, and I froze, temporarily forgetting all the chaos surrounding me. He smiled, and I smiled back. I wanted to be happy to see him. Under different circumstances, I would've. But seeing Harlan only made me think about Lux, which triggered my anxiety all over again. The conversation where he told me to tell him when I ran into one of his enemies replayed in my head. I knew it was my chance to tell him about my random run-in with Lux, but my lips wouldn't part when I approached him for some reason.

"Hey, beautiful," he greeted me with a kiss on the cheek.

"Hey. Is this for me?"

"Yeah. I thought I'd repay the favor and pull up on you at work to bring you lunch."

"Thank you," I said with as much gratitude as I could muster up without tearing up. "You don't know how much I needed this."

"Rough day?"

"You have no idea," I replied with a nod. "C'mon, let's go over here."

He followed me to the nurses' station and set the bag on top. Curious, I peeked inside to see my favorite sandwich from the deli across the street from the hospital. The aroma of warm sourdough bread, roasted turkey, and melted cheddar cheese wafted out, making my mouth water. I'd only mentioned it in random conversation, but the fact that he picked up on it made my heart swell. The thoughtfulness behind the meal made it special, not the meal itself. Amid my chaos, his kind gesture brightened my day. Jhene Aiko was right: everything sweet wasn't sugarcoated. I wrapped my arms around him to show my gratitude, inhaling his familiar scent—a mix of motor oil and cologne.

"How'd you know I'd be having a crazy day?"

"I didn't, but I figured it's the ER, so this shit is always hectic. I can't fix that, but I can fix your hunger."

A smile broke past my lips. "I promise you I'm going to devour this the first chance I get."

"Good. What time is your shift over?"

"I get off at midnight."

"Aight, bet."

"Why? What do you have up your sleeve?"

"Nothing. Why?"

"Mmhm. Okay."

"All I wanted to do was see your beautiful smile for a second. I'll get out of your hair and let you get back to it."

"Thank you again, baby."

I leaned against him, feeling the weight of my day lift while my body was pressed against his. Harlan had become my anchor, keeping me grounded in the midst of a storm. I'd been so caught up in the beeping monitors and urgency of my surroundings that being in his arms brought me the peace I didn't know I needed. He didn't have to speak. He didn't have to make me laugh. His presence alone was my sanctuary.

———

The clock struck midnight, and I grabbed my things from the nurses' station before heading into the well-lit employee parking lot. A yawn escaped my lips as I sailed out of the sliding doors. I was bone-tired, and my dogs were barking. Harlan's motorcycle, a sleek black beast with chrome accents, rumbled to life as he revved the engine. The sound echoed through the empty parking lot. My eyes popped wide. *I knew he had something up his sleeve.* I looked down at my scrubs. Luckily, I'd just changed into a fresh pair after my original ones had been stained with splotches of blood. I had on a cozy hooded jacket. My hair was pulled up in a messy top knot bun, and I'd traded in my contacts for glasses halfway through my shift. I was far from cute.

"What are you doing here?" I inquired as I approached his bike.

Instead of responding, he presented me with a helmet. "You trust me?"

I looked at the helmet in his hand and then back at his bike—the padded seat and chromed-out features. I'd never been on a motorcycle before. The idea of going on a midnight ride both thrilled me and put the fear of God in me.

I traded glances with Harlan. His eyes were the perfect combination of trouble and gentleness, a deadly recipe that made my heart thrum wildly.

"Come on, Lady Luck," he encouraged, his voice gravelly yet inviting. "I promise I'll bring you back in one piece. Plus, you told me you'd ride with me one day. That day is now. I swear, you'll feel the wind like you've never felt it before."

"Where are we going?" I quizzed nervously before accepting Harlan's wild invitation to ride into the unknown.

Harlan swung a leg over the bike, settling onto the leather seat. "Somewhere quiet, away from all the chaos of the city," he yelled over the engine's loud, masculine growl. "It's just you and me tonight."

I took a deep breath, feeling remnants of leftover adrenaline from my hectic shift coursing through my veins, and climbed behind him. We slid our helmets on, and I pressed my chest against his leather jacket while coiling my arms around his waist. He revved the engine before shooting forward, leaving the hospital in our rearview. I squeezed my eyes shut, clinging to Harlan as if my life depended on it.

Somewhere along the ride, I stopped being afraid. The chaos of the ER and my hectic day melted away. All I felt was the rush of the night. I opened my eyes, taking in the blurred city lights as we zoomed past. Soon enough, I leaned into the curves and enjoyed the wind whipping against my face. Harlan guided us through winding roads away from the city. He didn't have to say a word. The rhythm of the ride said it all. It was the perfect ending to my night.

We reached a hilltop overlooking the city, and Harlan killed the engine. Under the silvery moonlight was a picnic setup. He'd spread a soft blanket on the ground and surrounded it with dozens of flickering tea light candles and scattered pink and red rose petals.

"Baby, what is all this?"

He twisted his neck to look at me with a honeyed gaze. "A midnight picnic for you."

My gaze swept over the romantic scene—the candles, the petals, the traditional wicker picnic basket. Tears shimmered in my eyes. "But why? H-how?"

"Because you take care of mothafuckas all day. It's time for someone to take care of you," he declared before getting off his bike.

"Thank you for this," I whispered as he helped me down. "No one has ever done anything like this for me before. It's perfect."

"I'm not gonna lie and act like I was the mastermind behind all this. Mama helped me out. I don't have a romantic bone in my body, but I told her I wanted to do somethin' nice for you to take away your stress. So, she helped me get all this shit together last minute," he admitted.

I rested my head against his chest, listening to his steady heartbeat. "Please thank her for me."

"I will."

He guided me to the blanket, and we sat side by side. The flames danced under the cool night air. The scent of dew-kissed grass hung in the air as the moonlight peeked through clouds and stars winked above us. At that moment, I realized love showed up in the tiniest acts.

"How was the sandwich from earlier?" he inquired.

I cheesed proudly. "Demolished as promised."

"Well, I hope you're not too hungry. It's not much in this damn basket, but it's something."

My laughter mingled with the night breeze as I leaned forward to cup his face. "Whatever is in there is perfect."

He opened the picnic basket in the center of the blanket. Inside, he'd packed chocolate-covered strawberries, a bottle of sparkling cider, and two champagne flutes. Harlan poured the sparkling cider into the glasses, and we clinked them together.

"Here's to you, Lady Luck. Cheers."

I smiled. For once, I wasn't stitching up wounds or helping save lives. I was simply a woman being swept off her feet by a gangsta. "Cheers."

HARLAN

T*wo weeks later.*

My eyes cracked open to the growl of a motorcycle zipping past my bedroom window. It was five o'clock in the morning when my feet hit the floor. The sun hadn't risen, but parts of the city were already alive. My chest tightened as soon as I sat up in bed. I'd spent every day since my brother died living on high alert. *Who the fuck killed Low? Am I next? Which one of The Spades has the work? When is the next shipment coming in? Who's got the money for the re-up?*

Low would always tell me that you couldn't rest when you were at the top. And since I'd become president of The Spades, my days had become a tightrope walk between loyalty and ruthlessness. I'd been way too stressed. Clover was my calm amid all the chaos and my salvation. I'd always looked at love as a liability, but I'd ride the edge for her without question.

I knelt before our club's emblem beside my bed—a hissing viper coiled around a black spade, which represented rebellion, freedom, and death to our enemies. I lit a candle and watched the flame dance. The Spades were my family, their loyalty forged in blood. My lids closed as I whispered a prayer for protection from my enemies and justice for Low. I knew better than anyone that the streets were a battlefield.

I headed toward the kitchen after showering and dressing. Fully awake, I stood before the counter, staring at Low's leather jacket hanging over the bar chair like a sacred relic. Suddenly, my heart became heavy with memories—our childhood, the scent of motor oil, the low hum of engines in the shop. I reached for it. The leather was weathered, etched with stories—road trips, bar brawls, and brotherhood. It felt like history and loyalty passed down through blood. The patches were worn, threads frayed, but they still held the promise of honor and respect. I ran my thumb over our club emblem. It carried the weight of leadership.

I slipped my arms into the sleeves, allowing the jacket to mold to my skin and the weight of responsibility to settle onto my shoulders. It'd been months since the first time I slipped it on, and the weight was still both comforting and suffocating. The collar brushed against my tattooed neck, and I imagined Low's voice—the stern advice, the laughter after a wild-ass night, or a close call with the cops. My eyes slammed shut as I drew in a deep breath. For a split second, I'd been transported back to those hellish nights, speeding down the moonlit highways as the wind slapped my face.

"Goddamn, I miss you, bro," I mumbled, hanging my chin low.

His jacket fit me like armor. It was more than a piece of clothing; it was our legacy. I stepped over to the mirror stationed by the front door and stared at my reflection. There I was, the president. Yet, all I saw was Low's face staring back at me. I adjusted the collar and squared my shoulders before brushing my hands down the sleeves. I could feel his secrets etched into the leather.

"I'ma make this shit right before I leave the Chi, bro. I promise you that," I whispered before grabbing my keys and leaving the house.

Outside, the engine roared as I slid on my helmet and revved my bike. I peeled away from the curb with Low's jacket hugging me like a second skin. I knew I wasn't alone. Low was still riding with me in every stitch and every scar. The cool, early morning wind whipped through the patches as I leaned into the throttle. I whipped through the city, tires churning against the asphalt past neon signs, boarded-up shops, and alleyways.

———

My boots hit the ground as I walked into the clubhouse. The smell of sweat, brown liquor, and gasoline was in the air. The Spades—my brothers—were already there, their Black and Brown faces etched with scars and stories. They nodded as I entered, their respect unspoken but felt all the same. I was their leader, their bloodline. The clubhouse was our sanctuary, where our brotherhood was inked into the walls that held our secrets. I stood before them and presided over the morning meeting. Our club's business was ruthless—drug deals, turf wars, and unresolved vendettas. Still, our loyalty was sacred. The Spades were my family. They'd die for me, and I'd do the same for them.

"Any more new business before we move on?" I asked.

I filled my lungs with a deep breath after posing the question. As my final order of business, I planned to tell them about my upcoming move to New York. I'd been struggling with how to break the news to them and how they'd react, especially since none of them had met Clover except for Chop. Before I could gather my words, Shank, one of our low-level dealers, rose to his feet.

"I wanted to make sure the information was legit before I brought this to you and everyone else's attention." His voice was clear and direct as he spoke.

"What is it?"

"There's been a rumor buzzing around on the streets about Harlow's murder," he announced.

The room fell so silent you could hear a pin drop. My blood boiled instantly at the mention of my brother's murder.

"And what exactly are the streets sayin' that they ain't already said? Every lead we've gotten has only led to a dead end," I grunted.

"I got a witness. A Diablo Disciple."

My brow ticked up with curiosity. "Where?"

"Tied up at the warehouse, waiting for you to question 'em, kill 'em, whatever you want."

After hearing his news, I quickly decided to table my announcement. If there was *anyone* who had answers, I wanted to hear from them myself. Nothing would've made me happier than to get justice for my brother before kissing this fuckin' city goodbye.

"Well, let's go see what the fuck this pussy ass mothafucka has to say."

Before we rode out, I put the word out to Bricks to move our product around to different stash houses in the event of retaliation. I didn't want to take any chances. My phone buzzed just as I approached my bike. I looked at the screen to see an unread message from Clover.

Clover: *Hey. I tried calling, but your phone went straight to voicemail. I just wanted to let you know I'm going out with the girls tonight, and then I'll see you later. I love you.*

The last three words of her message threw my heart into high gear. I quickly pocketed the phone and made a mental note to hit her back after handling my business. I didn't have time for matters of the heart at the moment.

———

The Spades followed behind me, engines rumbling like thunder in the middle of a summer storm. My mind was a map of alliances and rivalries. All I could see ahead of me was more temptation, more problems, and a hell of a lot more fuckin' pain. The Diablo Disciples were our sworn enemies. They were always lurking in the shadows. And if I had to take them all out one by one to find out which of them had a hand in killing my brother, I would. I was going to carve my name on the inside of the skull of *whoever* took Harlow from me.

I arrived at the warehouse and marched inside with my crew at my back. The air inside the dimly lit space crackled with tension. I clenched my fist the minute I saw the rival gang member. His body was bound to a rusty chair, sweat trickling down his forehead. By the looks of it, he'd already taken a hell of a beating before I'd arrived. I stood tall and cracked my knuckles before marching over to him and ripping the duct tape off his lips. He winced in pain while letting out an agonizing scream.

"Ahh, shit," he hissed.

I clenched my jaw. "Tell me what the fuck you know."

"What? I-I don't know shit! I swear!"

"Y'know, it's been three months, and the cops *still* haven't solved my brother's murder? But you wanna know what I think? I think someone in *your* gang took my fuckin' brother from me."

His eyes darted around, fear etched into his expression. One look at him and I knew he was nothing but a pawn in a deadly game. "I don't know anything, man. It wasn't us."

I scoffed. "Bullshit. You think I believe that fuckin' shit? My brother's blood stains these streets, and I won't rest until I find the truth! So either you gon' tell me, or I'm gon' put a bullet in your fuckin' brain and drag your body through the mothafuckin streets!" I threatened as I circled him like a predator circling its prey. The concrete floor echoed my footsteps. "Harlow was a good nigga. Started this fuckin' club and kept it together. It's because of him that we allow you fuckin' pussies to share this city! And you fuckin' bastards took him out."

"Look, I'm just a soldier, aight? The orders came from above!"

"Orders? Orders from who?" I growled, grabbing his throat and pulling him close.

"B-before I say anything else, I-I want protection f-for me and my f-family from any retaliation from the Disciples. If they find out I snitched, they'll k-kill me, and you k-know it."

My grip tightened around his throat. "And what makes you think I won't?"

"P-please," he begged, choking.

"If it's protection from me you want, then that's what you'll get. Now speak."

No one was around to hear his bitch ass screams or him snitching on his supposed brothers. If his disloyalty showed me anything, it was that everybody wasn't the same niggas you grew up playing on the monkey bars with.

"Lux. He wanted control. Your brother stood in the way of that."

I knew that name all too well. He was the president of the Diablo Disciples. He'd hated The Spades for years and had a particular distaste for my brother. He was one of the first people I suspected after Low died, but he was supposedly out of town the night everything went down. I had it looked into it, and his alibi checked out. But if the word came from him, I'd make sure we'd have a word.

"Control of what? Why?" I growled.

"Power, nigga. It's *always* about power."

My gaze hardened. "Was he the one who pulled the trigger?"

He lowered his gaze. "I can't—"

"You can and you will. Or you'll be joining my brother in the afterlife."

"I thought you said I was protected!"

I smirked. "I told you that you'd be protected from me, not them," I explained, pointing my thumb at The Spades surrounding me, all armed and ready.

He hesitated before whispering his answer. "Yeah. It was him," he confirmed.

"Are you fuckin' sure? You better not be lying to me, nigga!"

"I'm not! I swear!"

"Crossing us was a mistake. I'ma make sure the asphalt drinks his fuckin' blood," I forewarned before cracking my balled fist against his jaw. "You're lucky my brother believed in redemption. I don't and neither do they," I hissed before walking off, leaving him for my brothers to tear to shreds.

The warehouse door creaked shut behind me, drowning out his screams. I finally had all the pieces to the puzzle and needed to form an airtight plan. Vengeance had taken root in my heart, and the hunt was on for Lux and whoever else from his crew that got in my way. I tossed my leg over my bike and let the engine hum before pulling off. I felt a war brewing in the breeze and knew my exit plan to leave for New York with Clover was the best move a nigga could ever make, especially after I killed Lux.

———

Later that evening, after the sun went down, I was on my way to my club's favorite bar, ready to toss back so much liquor my liver would *hate* me the next day when I saw flashing red and blue lights behind me.

"Fuck," I hissed as I slowed my speed and pulled over.

As the officer approached my bike, I slowly pulled my helmet over my head. "Put your hands in the air and get off the bike slowly," he ordered.

"Is all this necessary, Officer?"

"I said put your goddamn hands in the air and get off the fuckin' bike, punk!" he growled.

I shook my head while begrudgingly following his instructions. "All right, man."

"Now, put your hands behind your head and walk over there and put your hands on the wall."

I sucked my teeth. "Yo. Where is Chief Ramirez?" I called out, hoping to rattle him by name dropping someone above his pay grade.

Our club had an arrangement with the local police captain and a few dirty officers who looked the other way regarding our business in exchange for kickbacks and under-the-table funding for community initiatives like turkey and toy drives around the holidays.

"That's it, punk! I'm taking you in! You're under arrest!"

"What? On what charges?"

"How does possession of an illegal firearm sound?" He snickered as he yanked my hands behind my back and cuffed my wrists.

"What? That's bullshit, and you know it!"

"Tell it to the judge!" he responded as he marched me over to the back of his police car.

I scoffed. "This is cartoon-level fuckery. You know that? When I'm done with your ass, you're gonna wish your ass stayed on desk duty!"

"Is that a threat?"

"Nah. It's a fuckin' promise!" I hissed before he slammed the door in my face.

CLOVER

The red neon sign outside the bar flickered, casting an eerie shadow on the cracked pavement. My heart raced as my feet hesitated at the entrance. Quintessa and her sister had convinced me to join them for one last girls' night out before Harlan and I relocated to New York. Inside, the air was thick with cigarette smoke and the low hum of conversation. I followed Q and her sister to a corner booth, where the large speaker blared a hip-hop beat with a rumbling bass. My eyes surveyed the room—bikers in leather jackets with Diablo Disciples patches on them, tattoos of their insignia and other things etched into their brown skin like war stories. The place was one red flag after another.

"To Clover's last hurrah," Quintessa said, raising her glass. "To new beginnings!"

"Yassss!" Quiana chimed in with a wide smile.

I forced a smile to play along, but my mind was stuck on Harlan. He'd warned me about the Diablo Disciples. Their feud with Harlan's motorcycle club ran deep; from the looks of it, we were smack in the middle of their territory.

"I think we should hit up another bar," I suggested, feeling more uneasy as the minutes passed.

"Why? It's pretty lit in here."

"If it's my last girl's night out, I wanna bar hop."

Quiana nodded. "I'm down for whatever as long as I can keep drinking."

Quintessa, on the other hand, wasn't so willing. "I've got my eye on the cutie behind the bar, so I'm not tryna go anywhere no time soon."

I smacked my lips. "Fine. I'm giving you two more rounds of drinks to go speak to him. If not, I'm rolling out!"

"Whew! The pressure is on, sis. How you gon' act?" Quiana egged her older sister on.

"You can't rush perfection!"

"He's the bartender, Q! We'll be here *all* night if you wait for him to come up to you," I told her.

Quiana nodded before squeezing a lime between her teeth and tossing back a tequila shot. "She's got a point, sis."

Quintessa batted her long eyelash extensions while rolling her eyes toward the ceiling. "Whatever. Give me some more time to scope the place out. I don't wanna jump on the first thing I see either."

My chest deflated with a sigh. It was clear the night wasn't about me at all. Quintessa only asked me along as a poor excuse to go out for a chance to meet *her* dream guy. By the looks of things, it was going to be a long damn night.

———

As the night wore on, my uneasiness only continued to grow. The bikers eyeing me with predatory gazes didn't help either. It was as if I had Harlan's scent on me. Somehow, they knew I wasn't an ally.

"Hey, I gotta pee. Anybody wanna come to the bathroom with me?"

Quintessa had her eyes glued to the bartender while smiling like a giddy schoolgirl. "Huh?"

I kissed my teeth. "Nevermind. Quiana, you wanna go with me?"

Her face rumpled with confliction. "I would but my song *just* came on! I'ma shake my ass real quick, and then I'll come find you!" she promised.

I huffed before excusing myself from the table. "Fine. I'll be right back."

My pulse raced as I headed toward the restroom. It was only a few paces away, but it felt like miles. After relieving my bladder, I returned to an empty table. Q and her sister were gone, and so were their things. Panic coursed through me. *Did those hos leave me?*

Just as I turned to scan the room, a gloved hand clamped over my mouth. Before I could scream, I was being dragged toward the back exit. Panic clawed at my chest. It was fight or flight. I fought. I kicked. I swung while bellowing out muffled screams, but my masked captor was relentless. I was shoved into an unmarked van before the engine rumbled and sped away, leaving the bar's neon glow in the distance. Frantic thoughts raced through my head as I tried to understand every-thing. *Why me? What did they want?*

"P-please d-don't h-hurt m-me." I trembled. "I d-don't have any m-money! P-please l-let me g-go and I p-promise I w-won't s-say anything! I w-won't c-call the p-police!"

In the dim light, I caught a glimpse of one of my kidnappers as he bound my wrists and ankles together with zip ties. He was masked, but his eyes were like shards of icy glass. "We don't want money, bitch. We want your nigga."

My heart plummeted to the soles of my feet. His demand was chill-ing. *How do they know about my relationship with Harlan?* The van screeched to a halt before the door swung open. I was carried inside an abandoned warehouse where the walls whispered secrets of past gang violence and presented on my knees in front of the leader. I blinked rapidly, disoriented and afraid.

He removed his mask, revealing the familiar face with which I once shared family dinners. "Hey, sis."

My eyes ballooned as I looked up to see Lux staring back at me. "L-Lux?"

One of his goons who'd snatched me brought him my purse, and he turned it upside down in front of me, shaking out all its contents. He leaned forward to pick up my vibrating phone to ignore the incoming call before holding it up to my face to unlock it. I saw Quintessa's name across the screen and my heart almost leapt out of my chest.

"Call Harlan," he ordered. "Tell him to meet us here."

My voice cracked as I spoke. "Lux, p-please don't do this."

"This shit ain't personal. It's business. Now call him. Don't fuckin' make me tell you again," he snarled.

"M-my hands are tied," I reminded him, looking down at my bound wrists in front of me.

"Use your fuckin' voice recognition, Clover!"

My voice trembled. "Hey, Siri, c-call Harlan."

The minute it started to ring, Lux jabbed the speaker button to amplify the call. As panicked as I was to hear his voice on the other line, I became even more worried the longer the phone rang. Before I knew it, the call had gone to voicemail. Lux impatiently tapped his name again, reconnecting the call only to get the same result.

He paced the concrete, the Diablo Disciple tattoo of a skull crying red tears on his arm flexing. "This mothafucka better not be playin' no games," he growled. "Or I'mma have to turn shit up a notch."

Quintessa's name lit up the screen again and Lux angrily declined the call. I watched him tap a few buttons to block her number so he could free up the line for Harlan. As the minutes stretched into eternity, I couldn't help but wonder if love was enough. Harlan was a protector. I knew he'd do anything for me. The problem was Lux, and his goons seemed to know it too. Because I'd become the bait, Harlan would have to walk into the lion's den to save me.

HARLAN

I sat in the cold, sterile interrogation room, my knuckles raw from clenching. My leather jacket creaked against the metal chair. The bullshit charge—possession of an illegal firearm—was fuckin' laughable. But the police chief, Raymond Ramirez, had a reputation for playing hardball. I knew it was only a ploy to bring me in. My mind raced as I waited for him to come in and bring me my belongings.

He leaned back, studying me with his tired eyes that said *I'm over-worked and underpaid.* "You're a smart man, Harlan. I know you know why you're here," he acknowledged.

My jaw tightened. "I don't. How about you enlighten me."

His shoulders rose and fell. "I had to make it look convincing. Don't worry, we got your bike towed here."

I scoffed. "By getting one of your flunkies to bring me in on some childish ass charges? But since I'm here, we need to talk."

"I agree." Ramirez twisted his lips to the side before sliding a file across the table. "Lux came to me about our deal. He wanted in, the same arrangements and terms I had with The Spades for the Disciples. I didn't trust him. He and his crew were too reckless, so I told him no. I tried to shut him out, but he threatened warfare on the entire city. I couldn't afford an all-out gang war on my hands, Harlan. He wanted me to arrange a meeting with your brother to discuss terms."

"And you did it?"

He nodded. "The three of us had a sit down a month before Harlow's murder. Me, your brother, and Mr. Dorsey."

"What happened?"

"It was intense. Lux threatened to wage war if we didn't cut the Disciples into our deal. No amount of money would change his mind. So, Harlow put a separate deal on the table."

My brows creased. "What separate fuckin' deal, Ramirez?"

"He agreed to give the Disciples more territory in exchange for a truce. No war, no problem."

My pulse quickened. The Diablo Disciples were our venomous rivals—a gang that thrived on chaos, drugs, and bloodshed. I knew Harlow had a big ass heart, but if Ramirez's words were valid, the deal my brother made was a ticking time bomb.

"Why didn't Low tell me about this when it happened, and why are you telling me about it now?" I questioned. "After my brother was killed, I had you look into Lux Dorsey's whereabouts. You came back with information that his ass was out of the city when everything went down that night. Now, I have reason to believe your information was bogus. According to one of his own men, he was the one who pulled the trigger. You know anything about that?"

"I see you still haven't bothered opening the file in front of you," he replied.

I eyed him suspiciously before opening the manila envelope on the table. Inside were street camera surveillance photos from the night of Harlow's murder that put Lux in the city around the time things went down that night. I crumpled one of the photos up in my fist before swiping the rest off the table in a rage.

"Why the fuck would you fuckin' lie to me, Ramirez?" I roared.

"Take that bass out of your voice, Harlan. I lied because I knew the truce would be over if you knew the truth. We both know this city isn't big enough for both clubs."

"Why would Lux make a deal that worked in his favor only to cross my brother?"

"If I had to guess the motive, I'd say for power and the possibility to control more territory. I told you I didn't trust him then, and I still don't. God bless the dead, but Harlow was a fool to make that deal with a wildcard like Lux Dorsey. He's the type to do *anything* to come out on top."

"So why the fuck you tellin' me this shit now, huh?"

Ramirez's eyes held a warning. "Because I know what you and your boys did to one of the Disciples earlier today. Out of respect for your brother, I owe it to him to warn you that they're coming for you," he warned. "You're in danger, Harlan, and he won't stop until he's torn your entire club apart. Only a hound from the depths of hell can take him out. Watch your back."

I got to my feet, the chair scraping against the floor. "Don't worry about me. I'll handle it."

"Handle it how? By waging war?"

"The streets need a body for what happened to my brother, Ramirez. Ain't shit you can say to make me change my mind about that. I'ma handle this shit like I said, and then I'm leaving the city for good," I announced.

His hardened gaze bore into me. "For good? You think you can step down and leave it all behind?"

I shrugged. "I owe it to myself to try. Shit, I've been in this shit for what feels like a lifetime some days. Once I deal with Lux, I'm *done* for good. Like a ghost in the wind. Now get me my shit and let me do what the fuck I gotta do," I growled.

———

As I stepped into the hallway, the precinct's fluorescent lights flickered. Ramirez's news about Harlow's death still had my head spinning. I'd protect my club and get justice for my brother, even if it meant facing the Diablo Disciples head-on. I slid my phone out of my pocket. I hadn't checked it in hours. The officer who brought me in confiscated all my shit when taking me into custody. I tapped the screen to see dozens of missed calls from Chop. I pressed the phone to my ear while walking through the precinct doors.

Outside, the night air tasted like vengeance as I listened to Chop's desperate messages.

Chop's breath came in ragged bursts. *"Harlan,"* he huffed, *"Call me back, nigga. Nine-one-one. It's your girl, Clover. She's—the Disciples, they got her, man. They want you in exchange. Tell me what move you wanna make next."*

The world tilted as time slowed to a crawl. Clover, my Lady Luck—the one who'd stolen my heart with the soft skin and fierce brown eyes. The one who'd stood by me and wanted to build a future with me. She'd been kidnapped by the Disciples and was being held by Lux. Ramirez was right. The Diablo Disciples *were* coming for me and were using Clover as bait. If he laid one finger on her, I'd make sure they'd use it to identify his remains. I would go to hell and back if it meant saving her while making sure it was Lux's last fuckin' day on earth. I climbed onto my motorcycle—The Spades emblem gleaming on the tank as I dialed Chop's number, rage simmering.

"Harlan! Where the fuck are you?" Chop inquired when he answered, the urgency in his voice apparent.

"I got arrested and brought in by one of Ramirez's boys. I haven't had my phone on me in hours! What the fuck, man?" my voice growled, a mix of gravel and thunder. "How'd they get her?"

"Arrested? What the fuck? And I don't know. All they said was that they want you in exchange for her."

My racing thoughts competed with my erratic heartbeat. "Chop, it was Lux who pulled the trigger on my brother. Ramirez confirmed it."

There were a few seconds of silence on the other end of the phone. "Harlan. I know what you're thinking, and you can't—"

"I'll tear this entire fuckin' world apart behind that woman," I roared. "Clover's *mine*. And they'll all fuckin' pay for what they did to my brother, especially Lux."

Chop's voice was a plea. "Harlan, *think*. Revenge won't bring him back. Are you ready to start a war? You're the only one leaving the city when this is all over, not the rest of us."

His words fell on deaf ears as I disconnected the call. It didn't matter what he said or didn't say. Clover's life hung in the balance, and I'd rewrite the rules and ride straight into the heart of the storm for her.

Chop had been right about one thing. Revenge wouldn't bring Harlow back, but the streets of Chicago would bleed behind Clover, and the asphalt would bear witness.

My motorcycle roared to life. The road stretched before me—a twisted path of love, loyalty, betrayal, and revenge. I revved the engine, hoping the roar would help drown out my doubts and silence my emotions. I didn't move until my heartbeat was in sync with the engine. I promised myself I'd find Clover and make Lux pay. The Spades would rise, and the Diablo Disciples would fall. It would be the last thing I did before leaving the city for good and moving to New York with Clover.

CLOVER

My heart raced as I glanced around, assessing my surroundings, which smelled of dampness and desperation. The room was windowless, which made it feel like the cold concrete walls were pressing in. Thoughts galloped through my head, searching for an escape plan that wouldn't end with me or Harlan getting killed.

"Why? Why do this?" I asked Lux as my voice trembled while gripping my churning stomach. "Why not just kill me and be done with it?"

Lux shot me a chilling smile. "Because dead bitches don't lure their boyfriends into danger."

Fear clawed at my chest as I wiped the tears from my swollen eyes. "Fuck, Lux. I-I thought we were f-family!"

Lux's leather jacket creaked as he leaned against a rusted pillar. "Family?" he scoffed. "You stopped being my family when you started fucking my enemy."

"P-please, Lux. I didn't know you were enemies until recently!"

"I stayed cool with you out of respect for Lorenzo, but all is fair in love and war. Now, smile, Clo. We gon' send a pic to your boyfriend."

My hands trembled as I stared at the camera lens in front of me. The camera clicked, capturing my desperation. I could only imagine

Harlan's face when he received the photo. I couldn't bear to see another man I loved die on me. The phone rang, and my breath hitched, jarring my thoughts. The factory ringtone had a desperate melody in the heart of all the chaos. Lux picked up the phone and put it on speaker. His voice was chilling.

"It's about time you called back, mah'fucka."

"Listen carefully," Harlan threatened, his voice low and dangerous. "If you hurt her, I swear to God I'll burn this entire fuckin' city down and pick my teeth with your fuckin' bones."

Lux chuckled, the eerie sound echoing off the walls. "Feisty. I like that shit. But let's be clear, nigga. I won't hurt her unless I'm forced to," he replied, voice devoid of emotion.

"Forced?" Harlan roared. "You've already crossed that fuckin' line. It's me you want, right? Tell me where she is!"

Lux smirked, revealing a hint of cruelty. His sick ass was enjoying every second of it. "Patience, nigga. I'll text you an address. Come alone. No cops. No fuckin' tricks, or I might change my mind about hurtin' our little precious Clover."

"*Our*? Nigga, she's mine!"

Lux's cold gaze met mine. "Oh, he doesn't know how close we were, does he, sis?"

My eyes widened with panic. It was then that I realized just how twisted Lux's vendetta was. I was bait, a pawn in Lux's twisted game. "Lux! Please don't do this!" I called out.

"Sounds like you and I got some unfinished business to discuss once you pull up," he told Harlan.

"Send the fuckin' address!" Harlan roared into the receiver before ending the call.

My mind raced. I hadn't told Harlan anything about Zo's brother or his connection to his enemies, the Diablo Disciples. We were so close to leaving the city that I didn't think I had to. But the way Lux made it sound over the phone made it seem like I'd been lying to Harlan all along.

"Lux? Why would you say anything to him?" I hissed as fresh tears stung my eyes. "You think he'll fucking come for me now if he thinks I lied to him?"

"Trust me, that mah'fucka comin'. If anything, that nigga will probably come charging in quicker, thinking he can save you and demanding answers from me. That's when I'll pop his ass, just like I did his bitch ass brother."

My eyes popped wide. "Y-you killed Harlan's brother?"

He shot me a sinister smirk. "Guilty."

"Oh my God," I bawled. "Why, Lux? What the fuck is wrong with you?" I screamed.

"Because I know his bitch ass was the reason that fuckin' police chief wouldn't give my club the same protections he gave The Spades. Without it, the cops will keep picking my riders off the streets one by one. Meanwhile, those pussy ass Spades get to expand their territory while my niggas starve. So, I did what I do best: I waged war on *every fuckin' body*. Niggas started singin' a new tune after that. Harlow cut me in on more territory in exchange for a truce, only to fuck around and play with my money and my fuckin' respect!"

"I-I don't understand."

"He fuckin' played me, Clo! I had my niggas move in on the territory we agreed on, only for them to be ambushed by his niggas. He didn't tell them shit about our deal! Had me lookin' like a fuckin' fool in front of my crew! Those five bodies are on me! So, I made sure to get it back in blood by killing his fuckin' ass. You fuck me, I fuck you right back."

"You think Zo would be proud of you and all the shit you've done?"

Lux had lived on the knife's edge since I'd known him. Although he and Zo had grown up under the same roof, they were opposites. Lux's path was filled with stints of jail time and a laundry list of charges. Whereas Zo was a summa cum laude college grad with a pristine record.

His gaze lingered on me, memories etched in his expression. "I was born a demon. Zo knew that. He got all the good. My brother was the best part of our family. Never met a better man. His untimely death... God took him away too fuckin' soon."

"I wish things had turned out differently, too, but we can't change the past."

Lux looked at me with zero understanding in his eyes. "Yeah, because you've moved on, right?" He scoffed. "You could've fuckin' moved on with almost anybody else, Clo. Anybody else but him. I wouldn't have even been mad about it. I would've congratulated your ass."

"I've earned the right to move on with my life!" I yelled.

I'd mustered up all my energy to say those words and felt nothing but dizziness afterward.

My stomach rolled as bile threatened to spew. Suddenly, I was a ticking timebomb. "T-trash can! I need a trash can!"

Lux snickered. "Feeling sick, are we? Buck up, sis. This street shit ain't for the faint at heart."

"Please, Lux!" I begged. "I feel sick!"

He motioned to one of his henchmen, who brought over a plastic trash can. I clung to the edge of the trash can for dear life, retching as my stomach heaved. The room felt like a pressure cooker. All I could do was wonder *how* I'd gotten entangled in such a nightmare. Harlan, my beacon of hope, was more than likely walking straight into a trap—one set by someone I never thought would hurt me.

I wiped my mouth with the back of my hand while studying Lux. His fiery glare was devoid of any familial warmth. Lux had always been rough around the edges but had always been kind to me. He loved me like a big brother should've loved a sister. But the man who stood before me wasn't the one I once knew. He'd become something darker, more dangerous.

"When I found out you were dating that bitch nigga, Harlan, it felt like a slap in the face to me *and* my brother. You could do better. You've had better. So, I figured, what better way to make Harlan's ass suffer than to take you from him?"

My chest tightened. "P-please, Lux. I'm begging you, don't do this!" I screamed as tears raced down my face. "Just call it off! Call it all off and let me go!"

The room echoed with my desperate sobs as Lux watched, unmoved, before pulling out my phone again. "Don't worry, Clo. Your lil bitch ass boyfriend will be here soon. And then, my dear *ex*-sister-in-law, the real games will fuckin' begin," he promised before glaring at his henchmen who stood behind him like silent guards.

Harlan

The sound of Lux's crude laugh grated on my nerves as it replayed in my head like a broken record. My mind raced so fast I couldn't think straight. I gripped the phone so tight my knuckles turned white. I would've done anything to save Clover, even if that meant two-stepping with the devil himself. Mama would always say anyone worth falling for always came with a cost. And nine times out of ten, you always paid with your heart. Running after her without a plan was a guaranteed suicide mission. I needed a solid plan and the discipline to execute that shit without fail. I wouldn't be able to live with myself if something happened to Clover. As hard as it was to lock away my feelings for her, I knew I had to in order to do what I needed to do.

"This shit is real and banging at my fuckin' door, Low. Tell me what to do, bro," I mumbled while shifting my gaze to the sky.

I paced the floor, waiting for the text to arrive. As soon as it came through, I memorized the location—an abandoned warehouse on the outskirts of town. I grabbed my bulletproof vest and AK from the back of my closet and shot a text to Chop with the address, putting him on notice to round up the crew, strap up, and ride out. The city would tremble, and Lux and the Diablo Disciples would learn that The Spades and I were a storm they couldn't outride. I stepped outside and pulled my hood over my head. The rain fell in steady sheets, turning the city into a dark labyrinth. I popped the trunk on my Hellcat and put my AK in the secret compartment in the trunk before getting inside.

———

The warehouse loomed under the cool white light of the moon, rain drumming on its rusted roof. I retrieved my Glock from the glove compartment and slid it into the back of my jeans before grabbing my AK from the trunk. The misty night air was thick with tension as I stepped into the dimly lit warehouse, the heart of enemy territory. My knuckles clenched around the grip of the AK as my finger lay trained on the trigger. My heart was tight like a clenched fist, causing my breath to come in ragged bursts. The space smelled like dampness and vomit. And there, tied to a chair, was Clover—breathing and still alive. Her big, brown eyes widened when she saw me, her gaze a mix of relief and fear.

Before either of us could acknowledge the other with words, Lux and his goons emerged from the shadows with their guns drawn. Lux's face was twisted by greed. I scanned the space without moving my head. There were at least ten guns trained on me, making it clear I was outnumbered.

My fury burned hotter than hell. "I'm here, nigga. Release her," I demanded.

Lux's laughter echoed. "Oh, I will," he said. "But not before you and I have a lil chit-chat."

I kept my gun trained on him. "About what?"

"Lower your gun first. Staring at the barrel of your gun doesn't make me feel like this is a safe space."

I kissed my teeth. "You first."

He signaled for his men to lower their guns and I did the same. Lux's sneer was etched in hatred. "You owe me money on behalf of your bitch ass brother."

"Keep my brother's name out of your fuckin' mouth."

"Or what? You gon' cry? You soft as baby shit, nigga."

My rage surged as the angel and demon on my shoulders whispered competing actions in my ears. I gritted my teeth for restraint. "This shit ends tonight. Let her go, and you and I can settle whatever we gotta settle afterward."

"She's as much a part of this as you are."

My brows curled down. "What the fuck are you talkin' about?"

Once again, Lux's insufferable laughter echoed off the walls, causing my trigger finger to itch. "You think you know everything, don't you? Your precious Clover—she was engaged to my brother."

My world tilted as I shot my furious glare at Clover and was met with her pleading gaze. "H-Harlan!"

Lux's voice drowned her out. "That's right, baby boy. She's *my* family. You've had the Opps in your corner the whole fuckin' time. How does it feel, mah'fucka?" he taunted me.

"Don't listen to him, Harlan! That's not true!" Clover screamed.

I couldn't hear her. Not when the room erupted in gunfire. Something in me *clicked*. I'd gone from wanting to get Clover out safely by using the least amount of violence possible to shooting first and not planning to ask a damn thing after.

Lux's henchmen opened fire back, bullets tearing through the air. I dove behind a stack of crates, returning fire. The warehouse became a war zone—echoes of betrayal and love colliding.

Clover's wrists were still bound, her eyes wide with terror. "Harlan!" she screamed.

Her fearful screams pinched my heart. As betrayed as I felt, I still wanted her safe. I crawled to her, hands shaking as I freed her wrists. "Stay low!" I instructed.

The crates offered minimal protection. Splinters dug into our palms as we crouched down, waiting for a lull in gunfire. The moonlight sliced through the bullet holes in the windows, casting eerie patterns on the dusty floor.

"Harlan, I need to explain. About my past, about Lux and his brother," Clover whispered.

I stole a glance at her, and my spine stiffened. "I don't want to hear it. Not now."

But Clover persisted. "I swear it was innocent. After Zo died, we didn't talk that often, only check-ins or random run-ins. That's all!"

A stray bullet ricocheted off a nearby beam, sending sparks flying.

Clover flinched, her breath hitching as she slapped her trembling hand over her mouth to muffle her fearful screams.

"And you conveniently left out that he's your ex's brother after I told you about our beef with them?"

"I didn't want to upset you. We're just... I-I don't know... distant family."

I shot her an icy glare. "You can't be family with my enemies. Trust is the foundation of any relationship. You shattered that shit."

"Harlan, I want you! I love you!"

"You kept secrets from me, Clover, and now I doubt everything that comes out that fuckin' mouth of yours."

"Harlan, please! I'm sorry!"

Silence settled between us as the gunfire momentarily subsided. "We have to move," I whispered.

My grip tightened on Clover's shoulder as we darted from crate to crate, our shadows melding as one. Bullets whizzed past as I exchanged more gunfire.

My jaw clenched as I squeezed the trigger. I didn't want to hear her excuses or apologies. Not when one of the bullets hit my chest, igniting pain. "Ah, shit!" I hissed, dropping back a few steps before shooting back.

Clover's eyes doubled in size as she stood to spring into action. "Harlan!"

"Stay low!" I yelled just in time to see Lux aim his gun at Clover.

POW!

Clover's body jerked as she screamed. Her body crumpled to the floor. My heart fell with a bang. Time slowed, echoing our fractured bond. All my anger turned to panic before settling into a rage. My war cry echoed through the warehouse as I emptied my magazine into Lux's chest, each shot a scream of fury. His body crumpled against the ground. He gasped, blood pooling around him. I stepped up and fired the rest of the rounds from my Glock into him.

I spat on him. "That's for Low, you bitch ass nigga."

I dropped to my knees at Clover's side, cradling her in my arms while putting pressure on her wound. One look at all the blood, and I knew this was out of Doc's wheelhouse. She needed medical attention, stat. "Don't you dare fuckin' die on me, Lady Luck," I whispered to her. "Not after everything. I've got you. I won't lose you."

Her eyes fluttered. "I'm sorry," she gasped. "I love you."

My vision blurred with tears. "Shut up, yo. Just shut up. You gon' be fine."

I scooped her up, my adrenaline carrying us forward as I scanned the exit ahead. Lux's few remaining men were closing in, their jumbled footsteps echoing like the Devil's drumbeat. I raced outside and heard the familiar sound of engines roared in the distance. The Spades were on their way to finish what I started. I eased her into my passenger seat. The city blurred past as I sped to the emergency room. Her blood soaked my shirt, but I didn't care. As the rain intensified, my gaze met hers.

"I love you, too."

———

Doctors and nurses swarmed like bees to a hive around the ER at the hospital where Clover worked. I'd brought her there, hoping she'd receive the best care possible. I watched, helpless, as they wheeled her to the back. My anger had turned to something deeper—a raw ache that threatened to consume every ounce of me. I collapsed in a chair in the waiting room. The walls closed in as my mind raced. I'd vowed to protect and love her fiercely and failed. All I could do was pray for her life and forgiveness. An hour and a half later, a doctor emerged.

"We were able to remove the bullet fragments from her collarbone and shoulder. She's stable and expected to recover fully," he announced.

I nodded as tears of relief and joy threatened to stream down my face. I'd almost lost her; the woman caught in a war not of her making.

"Thank you, Doctor. Can I see her?"

"She's being moved to a post-op room on the fifth floor and will still be out from the anesthesia. Plus, visiting hours are over. Come back first thing in the morning," he informed me.

My chest deflated with a hard sigh. I would let her rest, and whenever she woke up, I'd tell her the truth: that I loved her, and I'd fight for her until my dying breath. I stalked through the automatic emergency room doors and back into the rain. After folding my body back into my car, I texted all club members, calling an emergency meeting. It was past time I came clean to them about Clover and my intentions to move away with her as soon as she was well again.

————

I marched into the dimly lit clubhouse and stood before the rugged assembly of my leather-clad riders. My gaze swept the room.

"Listen up," I began, my voice, usually stern and commanding, wavered with emotion. "I've got somethin' to say." The crew leaned in, eyes narrowing as they waited for me to explain. I knew my decision to leave would ripple through our brotherhood, but I couldn't put off my announcement any longer. "I'm stepping down as president. Effective immediately," I announced.

Murmurs erupted amongst them. I heard a voice call out from the crowd. *"What the hell? You're our backbone."* I traded glances with Chop, who scratched his beard. He was the first to know about my plans. I knew he felt a way about me leaving, but he respected my decision.

"He's got his reasons," Chop stated, having my back.

My jaw tightened as I nodded. "Clover, my girl, took a bullet for me. She's in the hospital right now, recovering."

Ghost, the treasurer, raised an eyebrow. "A bullet? Damn. You two gonna tie the knot now?"

My heart clenched. Wedding bells? It wasn't like the thought hadn't crossed my mind. "Maybe," I answered, surprising myself. "She's worth it."

The room fell silent. The Spades respected loyalty, even if it led them away from the asphalt and into uncharted territory.

Nitro, the club's road captain, cleared his throat. "We'll miss the hell out of you, but you gotta do what's right."

I dipped my chin. "Clover's my future, and New York's our next chapter. We'll leave the city together as soon as she's better."

Taz, the enforcer, grunted. "We'll always be brothers, mah'fucka. No matter the number of miles between us."

I dapped each one of them up, leaving Chop for last. "You know I got you," he whispered in my ear.

And with that, I walked away from the presidency. The Spades would carry on, and so would I, with a life beyond the roar of engines and the promise of something better. In time, I knew Clover's wound would heal, but the scars would always remind us of the battles we'd fought and the sacrifices we'd made to be together. Soon, we'd build a life together in the city that never sleeps. We'd leave the motorcycle club and the blood-soaked streets of Chicago in our rearview.

———

I returned to the hospital, eager to get an update on Clover. I knew there was a chance she was resting, but I couldn't wait until the next morning. I didn't care if I had to camp outside her door, the waiting room, or the parking lot. I wasn't going to be far away when she needed me most. My heart raced, each passing step echoing the urgency that had brought me there. I rounded a corner and nearly collided with a nurse. Her uniform was crisp, and the badge clamped to her chest read "Quintessa". Her kind brown eyes studied me for a moment.

"H-Harlan?" she inquired.

That's when I recognized her as Clover's friend. I'd only laid eyes on her briefly the night Clover backed into my car in the parking lot.

I swallowed hard, my voice barely audible. "H-hey. Wassup?"

"Are you here to see Clo?" she asked, assessing the desperation etched into my expression. "I've been so worried! What happened to her?" she asked gently. "One minute she was going to the bathroom and the next, she completely disappeared. I kept calling her phone until it started going straight to voicemail."

I hesitated for a split second, the memory of chaos and gunfire still fresh in my mind. "Wrong place, wrong time," I replied. "She took a bullet, and it never should've fuckin' happened!"

She held up her chocolate brown hands, palms facing upward to calm me. "Okay, okay. You look like you've been through a lot. Have you been seen? Are you hurt?"

"No. I'm fine. I'm not worried about me. All I wanna do is see her for myself, and once I know she's okay, I'll leave. Can you tell me what room she's in?"

Her brow furrowed, but she didn't press further. Instead, she glanced down the hallway. "Visiting hours are over," she said. "But I'll make an exception. Wait here. Let me go to the nurse's station and look up her room number. I'll be right back."

I nodded, grateful beyond words. "Thank you."

Quintessa disappeared then reappeared moments later. "She's on the fifth floor in room fifty-seven-thirty-one."

"Thanks."

"But I should warn you, when I saw her name on the OR board, I called her parents. They're already here."

"Fuck."

"I'm sorry."

"It's okay. Thank you for your help."

I stepped out of the elevator onto the fifth floor. Room numbers blurred past as I trekked down the fluorescent-lit hallway. My heart raced from the urgency of the situation and the impending confrontation I foresaw with her parents when I saw them standing outside her door. Worry and anger were etched into their expressions. Clover's mother's eyes were red-rimmed as she clutched a tissue in her trembling hand. Her father's face was stern but weary. He looked like he hadn't slept. They both turned to me with gazes sharp and accusatory. *Fuck. Here we go.*

"What are *you* doing here?" Clover's mother asked, voice brittle.

I swallowed hard. I hadn't had time to rehearse the moment, but there we were. "I came to see Clover," I replied, keeping my tone steady and respectful. "I want to be here when she wakes up."

Her father's jaw tightened. "You? You're the reason she's lying in that bed!" His finger jabbed toward the room where Clover lay. "She wouldn't have been caught up in this if it weren't for you!"

I clenched my fists, fighting the urge to defend myself and put her fuckin' pompous ass father in his place once and for all. But blacking his eye would only strengthen the narrative he already had in his head about me. I was nothing but trouble in his eyes. And because I was the reason his daughter took a bullet, he had more than enough reason to hate my black ass. I didn't know what all he knew about what went down or what he *thought* he knew. I didn't care. As much as I wanted to, I couldn't change what had happened.

"With all due respect, sir, I'm crazy in love with your daughter," I answered. "I'd never intentionally put her in danger."

Clover's mother scoffed. "Love? You think love excuses everything? Our daughter was safe until she met you. Now look at her! My baby is in a hospital bed!"

"I'm not leaving," I stated, voice firm. "If she wants me to leave, I'll wait for her to wake up and tell me."

"You're not her family," her father spat. "You have zero right to be here!"

I shifted my gaze toward the closed door, knowing Clover was on the other side. "I love her," I repeated. "And I'm not leavin' her."

"You will, or we'll have security show your ass out!" her mother threatened.

Her father's brow furrowed. "Just go!"

"All I want to do is see her... *please.*"

Her mother's cold gaze softened as she reached for her husband's hand. "Give him two minutes," she whispered. "That's all his ass gets."

He nodded reluctantly. "Fine. But don't think this changes shit!"

My heart somersaulted in my chest as I stepped into the room. I pulled a chair close to Clover's bedside, keeping my gaze trained on her. Her parents followed me, lingering near the doorframe with obvious disapproval etched into their hardened expressions. As the seconds passed, I sat there, watching the rise and fall of her chest while lacing her fingers with mine. Regret gnawed at me.

"I'm so fucking sorry, baby," I whispered to her.

I wondered if she could hear me or even feel my presence. I lowered my head, silently whispering promises and apologies while praying her eyes would open and she'd wake up.

Her father approached me from behind, towering over me as I held her hand. "Time's up. Get the hell out of here and don't bring your ass back," he growled amongst the beeping of her machines.

I stood, ready to put my hands on his ass when the nurse sailed into the room. I shot a cold glare at Clover's parents. They were still there, still hating, but I didn't give a fuck. All I wanted Clover to do was wake up so I could see the forgiveness in her eyes.

"You heard my husband; get out now!" Clover's mother hissed.

"Ma'am, is everything okay?"

I tossed up my hands in surrender. "We good. I was just leaving, but trust me, I won't be far away," I promised.

CLOVER

My eyes fluttered open to see a sterile hospital room. Only this time, I was the one in the bed instead of the one providing treatment. The room was cheerless as the beeping of machines punctuated the silence. I slowly lifted my hand to rub my eyes, hoping to clear the blur. The air was heavy with tension as I looked to see my parents sitting by my bedside. Their faces were etched with anger and concern.

"W-what happened?" I asked groggily.

My father shot to his feet. "Princess! How are you feeling?" he probed, stroking my head like I was five years old again.

"We came as soon as we heard, baby girl. You suffered a gunshot wound to your collarbone with some injuries to your left shoulder," my mother informed me as she slowly rose from her seat.

"H-how did you two know I was here?"

"Your friend Quintessa. As your emergency contacts, we were still in the system, so she reached out. She said she'd been worried sick after you all went out and she couldn't find you at some bar. Do you remember what happened?" my father inquired.

Flashbacks of the last twenty-four hours rippled through my mind, and my eyes slowly widened. "H-Harlan. W-where's Harlan?"

My parents exchanged glances before my father spoke up. "He's gone, Clover. He's not good enough for you."

"What did you say to him? Where'd he go?" I questioned while trying to sit up in bed.

My father reached out to stop me. "Clover, please calm down, princess. You're injured."

"Where is he?" I persisted.

"We sent him away," my mother finally answered.

"And like I told your parents earlier, I ain't goin' nowhere," Harlan stated as he entered my hospital room.

"I thought my husband and I told you to leave!" my mother hissed. "*Our* daughter is lying in a hospital bed with a gunshot wound because of you!"

"Because of your recklessness!" my father added, rage furrowing his brow.

Harlan stood at the foot of my bed with his jaw clenched. "I'm the one who saved her, damn it! I put it on my brother. I would've taken the bullet for her if I could."

"You're *not* good enough for our daughter. Stay the hell away from her!" my father warned.

"She deserves better," my mother jabbed, ensuring her negative comment was inserted into the conversation.

"With all due fuckin' respect, Mr. and Mrs. Baldwin, she's made her choice. We're in love, and nothing—"

My father's light brown complexion started to redden. "Get your ass out of here before I call security!"

"I'm not leaving unless Clover tells me to," Harlan replied, voice steady as he stood firm.

"That's it!" my mother roared before storming out of the room.

"Mom! Please!" I called out, but my voice was too weak. I was still too groggy from the pain meds to defend Harlan the way I wanted to.

"He needs to leave, princess! It's time for you to let his Black ass go!" my father insisted.

Harlan sucked his teeth as he continued to stand ten-toes down with determination etched into his cinnamon-brown features. Before he could react, my mother returned with two security guards. Their uniforms were stark against the sterile walls.

"Sir, you need to leave," one told Harlan as the other reached for his arm.

Harlan jerked away. "Neither one of you mothafuckas better put your fuckin' hands on me!" he roared.

All I could do was sit there and sob. The most important people to me couldn't stand one another. "H-Harlan, p-please g-go," I cried, feeling as helpless as a lamb.

Harlan continued to snatch away from security while approaching the door as they escorted him out. He kept his eyes locked on mine. "I love you, Clover," he called out before my mother slammed the door behind them.

"H-how could the two of you d-do t-this to me?" I sobbed. "I love him!"

Before either of them spoke up, a doctor walked in with a clipboard. "Good afternoon, Ms. Baldwin. I'm Doctor Harris, the attending physician. Can I please speak with you privately?"

I shot my parents a look before they stepped out, leaving me alone with the doctor. He stepped forward and paused at my bedside.

"What is it, Doc? Is something wrong?"

"Your surgery went well, but we discovered something else."

"What is it?"

"It looks like the gunshot wound isn't the only thing that's about to change your life. *You're pregnant*, Ms. Baldwin," Doctor Harris confirmed with a nod.

My breath hitched as the room started to spin. "W-what?"

My mind flashed back to my run-in at the pharmacy with Lux. His unexpected presence had me so worked up that I'd left without getting the Plan B pill. *Shit.* With our move to New York right around the corner, I knew the news of a new baby would throw a serious wrench into our plans, more than a gunshot wound to the shoulder ever would. I didn't know how Harlan and my parents would react to the news of my pregnancy, but it looked like I was about to be the bearer of some very unexpected news.

———

A few minutes after Doctor Harris left, Quintessa stepped in clutching a bouquet of daffodils. The doctor's unexpected news echoed in my mind as my emotions swirled around inside me like a carousel. I was a tangled ball of fear, excitement, and uncertainty. Quintessa crossed the room, looking at me with tears in her eyes. I was sure the news of my injury had spread like wildfire amongst the hospital staff. We'd both seen trauma before, but this time was different. She was my friend, my confidante. We'd shared laughter over dozens of coffee breaks and shared secrets during graveyard shifts.

"Hey, Clo. How are you feeling? I've been torn between smothering you with attention and giving you your space to process."

"I think I'm in some sort of paralyzing shock, actually."

Quintessa placed the daffodils on the windowsill before snapping her neck in my direction with a crinkled brow. "Huh?"

"I'm freaking the fuck out right now, Q."

She raced to my bedside. "What? Why? Is everything okay? Do you need me to get the doctor?"

"No. No. The doctor just left. H-he j-just told me…"

Q leaned in closer. "Told you what, Clover? Dear God, please don't say it's a tumor or terminal cancer or something!"

I took a deep breath. "No. He said I'm pregnant."

My words hung in the air, heavy with implications. The dazed look on her face let me know her mind was racing at the same speed as mine. I'd gone from the strong-willed nurse who had taken a bullet, to now facing a different kind of battle, a tiny, fragile life blooming inside me.

She reached for my hand and gave it a quick squeeze. "Are you… serious?"

I nodded. "Yeah."

"What are you going to do?" she asked softly.

My fingertips traced the edge of the blanket. "I don't know. I never thought… I mean, I'm not ready. But can anyone ever be ready for this?"

"Well, you're not alone. I'ma be here with you through it all, girl. The late-night cravings, shopping for adorable baby clothes, and everything in between from here all the way to New York. We'll make it work!"

My gaze shifted to the window, sunlight streaming through. "I'm scared, Q. I'm about to start this new job in a whole new state. Plus, I haven't told Harlan. I feel like I still need time to process it. It's overwhelming, you know? Especially with everything else going on."

"That's completely understandable. You've been to hell and back, Clover."

My eyes filled with tears as all the traumatic thoughts flooded my mind. "I still don't understand."

Quintessa sat on the edge of the bed. "You're alive, and that's all that matters. And guess what? You're going to be an amazing mom! I've seen you handle tough situations day after day with poise and strength. Look at this baby as a new chapter in your life story."

I sighed. "I never thought I'd be sitting in a hospital bed contemplating motherhood. Like, what if I tell Harlan and he's not happy about it? Our relationship is still so new. This baby could make or break us."

"I'm sure you two will figure it out. I talked to him in the waiting room. That man adores you, Clo."

My hand trembled as I reached for the glass of water on the bedside table. "You should've seen him, Q. The way he saved me, put his life on the line for mine. I thought I was going to die."

"Do you feel up to talking about what happened that night when we were at the bar?"

I lowered my gaze. "It's all a blur, really."

"You said you were going to the bathroom and then we never saw you again. I was blowing up your phone and then when I saw your name on the OR board for surgery I almost lost my mind!"

"Yeah. My parents told me you called them."

Q's chest deflated with a long sigh. "Again, I'm just glad you're okay. We've both seen our share of accidents and illnesses, but seeing you in this hospital bed, this hits different."

"Yeah, I know."

"I brought you those daffodils. The lady in the gift shop told me they're supposed to brighten up the room."

My lips twitched into a half-smile. "They're beautiful. They remind me of spring. Thank you, Q."

She nodded. "Fitting for your new beginnings."

I watched her get up to cross the room and open the blinds, allowing the natural sunlight to flood the room. Dust motes danced in the golden rays, and for a split second, my hospital room felt less depressing.

Still, I winced as the bright light touched my face. "Why did you have to open the blinds, Q?"

"Because we need a little sunshine in here. And besides, we're celebrating! You're alive and you're having a fucking baby!"

Fresh tears filled my eyes. "It looks like I'm going to be a mother."

Harlan

Two days later.

I leaned against the hood of my Hellcat, smoking a blunt in the hospital parking lot, when I spotted Clover stepping out into the weak sunlight with her wound bandaged. Her friend, Quintessa, was waiting by the exit. Clover greeted her with a smile before leaning on her steady arm as they approached the lot. I immediately put out my blunt and pressed toward them. Clover froze when she saw me. I approached, gaze never leaving hers. I knew I looked and felt like a man who'd been to hell and back, but I was there for her. Quintessa instinctively stepped back, giving us space.

"I had to make sure you were safe," I explained, voice raw with emotion. "I told you I'd always protect you and failed."

Tears welled up in her eyes. "Harlan, don't. It wasn't your fault."

My jaw clenched as I my face screwed into a scowl. "You never should've been put in the middle of that shit."

"He told me what he did to your brother. I'm *so sorry*, Harlan. I swear to you. I didn't know he had anything to do with it until he told me at the warehouse. But I should've been upfront with you when I found out about the tension between your club and Lux. I should've told you who he was to me, or at least who he *used* to be," she said, voice breaking. "The bottom line is, I don't blame you. I love you."

My heart twisted. Our rivalry had escalated into violence, and she'd been caught in the crossfire. A gunshot wound was a small price to pay for surviving, but the guilt behind it gnawed at me. My desperate eyes searched hers. "I love you too. More than anything."

"There's something else. Something I need to tell you."

My brow furrowed. "What is it?"

Clover took a deep breath. "I'm pregnant."

Her words shifted my entire world. She'd dropped a hell of a bombshell on me. The thought of new life, of a tiny heartbeat growing inside her, softened me. After all the deaths I'd seen, the bloodshed and the brotherhood, I couldn't help but smile. "For real?"

She nodded. "Yeah."

I swallowed hard. "How do you feel about it? Y'know, becoming a mother?"

She shrugged with her good arm. "I don't know. I've had less than forty-eight hours to digest the news and still feel a whirlwind of emotions. I'm excited and terrified. Every time I close my eyes, I imagine ten tiny fingers and toes, the late-night feedings, the weight of new responsibility... But underneath it all, there's this flutter in my heart that won't go away. Like, I can't get over the fact that there's a life growing inside me."

"Yeah. Me either."

"What about you? We haven't talked about kids before now, and with the move and my new job, it's not the *ideal* time for any of this."

"I thought I taught you it was okay to color outside the lines sometimes."

She smirked. "Shut up."

"Listen, after you got shot, I told my crew that I was stepping down as president of the club and that you and I were leaving this city. And with Lux out of the picture, we can live a life away from the chaos. You took a bullet, Clover, and you're carrying my seed. I don't want your sacrifice to be in vain."

Clover slowly reached out to touch my cheek as a tear slipped down her cheek. "Harlan, I want our child to grow up in a world where love triumphs over violence."

I nodded before brushing my lips against hers. It felt like forever since we'd touched. I missed the feel of her, her smell, her warmth, everything. "It will. I'll make sure of that."

We stood in the hospital parking lot embracing, wounded but hopeful. Even in the darkest times, life had found a way to surprise me with a second chance to heal, love, and build something worth fighting for with the woman I loved.

I slipped her hand in mine. "Ready to go home?" I asked, voice gentle as I kissed her forehead.

She squeezed my hand. "Yes, please."

"You feel up to riding with me somewhere?"

"Where?"

"It's a surprise. You trust me?"

"With my life," she replied.

"Let's go, then."

"Okay. I'll call Q and let her know I'm leaving with you."

I helped Clover into the car, ensuring her movements were slow and careful. I tucked her hospital discharge papers in my pocket as the weight of our secret news pressed against my chest. A smile came to my face as I imagined rubbing her growing belly and swollen feet after a long shift at the hospital.

As I drove through the familiar Chicago streets, Clover's eyes widened. "Where are we going?"

I grinned. "I thought you said you trusted me."

"I do."

"Then relax, Lady Luck. You'll see."

I'd been toying with the idea of taking her to see my mother, knowing it would be the perfect way to lift Clover's spirits after everything that had gone down. My mother adored Clover. In her eyes, she was the daughter she never had. She'd been asking about her and praying over her ever since she'd been in the hospital. A visit with my two favorite girls was sure to brighten both of their days.

————

Twenty minutes later, we pulled up to a cozy house with a modest front yard and a white picket fence. The garden was in full bloom, and the scent of lilacs hung in the air. I helped Clover out of the car, and we walked up the path together.

My mother opened the door, and her eyes widened in surprise. "Harlan! Clover! What a wonderful surprise!"

Clover smiled weakly. "Hi, Mrs. Banks."

She pulled us both into tight, warm hugs. "None of that 'Mrs. Banks' nonsense. Call me Marie."

We stepped inside, the warmth of the house enveloping us like an embrace after a long, hard day. Mama led us into the living room, where old family photos adorned the walls.

"Sit, sit," Mama insisted, eyes shining with joy. "Tell me everything. How are you feeling? Are you ready for your big move to New York?"

I exchanged glances with Clover. The news of her pregnancy still hadn't set in, but with Mama's kind eyes on us, it felt all too real.

"I'm recovering," Clover answered. "And as far as New York, I think we're as ready as we're gonna get."

Mama beamed, eating it all up. "New York is a big step. I'm so proud of you both."

Clover fidgeted with her hands before lacing her fingers with mine. "Actually, there's something else."

I squeezed her hand, silently giving her the green light to share the news. "I feel like we've been silently going back and forth about it since we got here, but we've decided to tell you."

Mama leaned forward, eyes wide with curiosity. "Tell me what?"

Clover drew in a deep breath. "I'm pregnant," she announced.

"With your first grandchild," I added.

Mama's eyes popped wide as she froze. Time seemed to stop for her as she stared at us with tears welling up in her eyes. Seconds later, she burst into tears, pulling us both into a hug. "Oh my God! A baby! Are you two serious? I've been praying for this!"

Seeing all the joy in her eyes and hearing it in her voice made my heart swell up ten times over. "You're the first person we've told."

Mama wiped her tears. "God bless you both. A baby. Oh! My heart can't take it," she squealed, splaying her fingers against her chest.

I sat in the presence of my two favorite girls, feeling like I was in Heaven. Mama's prayers had been answered, and Clover's sacrifice had brought us to that moment with the promise of new life.

———

Clover and I spent the next few hours with my mama, listening to her share stories of my childhood and tossing around potential baby names for her first grandbaby. After dropping Clover off at her place to rest, I headed out to do one more thing before settling in for the night.

The cemetery stretched out ahead of me in the dim light of the late afternoon. I studied the area. It was a somber sheet of weathered tombstones and memories carved into the soil. The faint scent of roses wafted past my nose before I noticed the crimson petals scattered across the ground like hushed secrets.

My heart dropped with sadness as I stood at my brother's grave. He was a man of grit and loyalty. It was that same loyalty that cost him his life.

The wind whispered through the tall oak trees as my fingers traced the engraved letters on the headstone. "Low," I murmured. "I know you probably wondering why I ain't came to visit your ass. The truth is, I couldn't face you. Not until I got justice for you, bro. You always said loyalty was everything. Look where it fuckin' got you, you stubborn mothafucka."

My voice cracked, raw with emotion. I teared up, becoming visibly upset as I settled into my grief. I imagined Low's gruff laughter, the way he'd slap his hand on my shoulder and say, *Don't cry for me, lil nigga. Sometimes, loyalty is all we got.*

But being there and staring at his grave only made loyalty feel like a noose around my fuckin' neck. I'd stayed in the city long enough to bury my brother and honor him in blood as our fallen president, but I couldn't bear the weight of the patch on my back anymore.

"I'm leaving the Chi. Leaving the chaos, the bloodshed. There's a girl—a beautiful fuckin' hell of a woman, actually. She's the one, yo. She's got a nigga believin' in something beyond this life."

I felt his spirit with me as I imagined him raising an eyebrow with skepticism in his eyes. *In love? You, nigga?*

"Yeah," I said, voice steady as if we were conversing. "Her name's Clover, but I call her Lady Luck. She's got the same fire in her veins as I do, but she's good. She's seen so much darkness, and she's still as pure as snow. We're leaving all this shit behind and moving to New York to build something real."

I knelt, pressing my palm to the damp earth beneath my boots. "I wish you could've met her, Low. She's got a laugh that could light up the night and these beautiful big brown eyes that see through all the bullshit. She's real. She's home. She's my redemption, my second chance at something better."

The wind carried my words away, and I stood, wiping tears from my eyes. "I got a lil one on the way. A nigga about to become a fuckin' family man and shit. Can you believe it? I wanna be happy about it. I *am* happy about it. It's just... when anything good comes my way, you are still one of the first people I think about. Some days, it still doesn't make sense why you're not here. My life will never feel complete without you here, Low. *Never*, my nigga. If it's a boy, I'ma give him your name. You'll live through me and my seed. You'll never be forgotten, my G," I whispered, brushing dirt from the headstone.

"Rest easy, Low," I told him.

And with that, I turned away from my brother's grave, laying his leather jacket in front of his headstone instead of flowers. I'd always carry his memory with me, but I wouldn't continue to let it shackle me to the city. Ahead lay the open road, and with my Lady Luck by my side, there wasn't a doubt in my mind that we wouldn't find peace. Our bond could heal the deepest wounds.

As I went on my away, I imagined Low's gruff voice one last time. *"Gon' find your peace, lil nigga. I've found mine."*

Epilogue

C lover
Six months later.

The bright morning sun cast speckled shadows on the path as Harlan and I strolled through Central Park. He liked it because it felt like home away from home, mirroring Millennium Park back in the Chi. It'd been six months since we'd left Chicago behind and started anew in New York. We'd traded deep-dish pizza for cheesecake and the *L* train for the subway. It was safe to say I'd fallen in love with the city. On the other hand, Harlan took a while to warm up to the transition, but he'd made the best of it for me. He spent the first few months traveling back and forth to Chicago, checking in on his mom, the shop, and the motorcycle crew.

Whoever said New York never slept was right. The hospital I worked at was always bustling with an influx of new patients, keeping my nursing skills in high demand. It was crazy, but I loved the energy of New York and the way it pushed me forward. When it came time to renew my contract, the hospital agreed to extend me throughout my pregnancy. I liked where I worked, and I'd found an excellent doula I trusted to deliver our baby girl when the time came. Harlan placed a hand on my growing belly, which had seemed to swell overnight. With each kick, I felt the promise of new beginnings, which always made me smile.

"So," he began, "baby names. Got any favorites yet? We ain't got but so much time left," he stated as if I didn't know I had a bun in the oven.

I chuckled. "We've still got three whole months to decide, baby! But I've been thinking. How about Aria? It means song or melody."

"Aria sounds too soft for my baby girl. I already know she's gon' be a fierce lil soul and beautiful as hell."

I smiled. "The way these kicks are rolling in, you might be right about that. Baby girl can pack a punch."

His gaze softened as he smiled, eyes crinkling at the corners. "See. I told you."

"What do you like then?"

"Brave," he answered.

My eyebrows shot toward my hairline. "Brave?"

"Before you shut it down, hear me out. I already told you she's gonna be fierce like her daddy and have a lion's heart like her mother. I think Brave is a perfect fit."

I nodded. "Brave Sarai Banks. Sarai means princess, so it's strong yet royal." We passed a group of joggers, their sneakers pounding the pavement as they zoomed by us. I pressed my hand to my stomach when it rumbled. "Speaking of strong, I'm hungry. Where do you wanna go for breakfast?"

"Your ass is always hungry. Our little girl must be growing like a skyscraper in there."

I playfully rolled my eyes. "Whatever. But seriously, I need nourishment. I'm thinking bagels, maybe? Or pancakes? Or French toast? I can't decide."

"How about we head back to that diner we hit a few weeks ago? You remember the one we had to run into because your ass had to pee?" he asked with a chuckle.

I chuckled, thinking about that smoky bar and how far we'd come.

"Shut up! You know my weak bladder is how we met in the first place! Besides, that place did have some good food."

"Right. Plus, it has that old-school nineties vibe."

My eyes brightened just thinking about their breakfast menu. "Sold. Maybe I'll have a stack of pancakes with a side of French toast and crispy bacon."

He laughed, the sound echoing through the park as we trekked down the block toward the diner. "Whatever my Lady Luck wants, my Lady Luck gets," he replied, slipping his arm around my waist. "I love you and our little one."

I leaned into him, the baby bump nestled between us. "We love you, too," I replied before pecking his lips. "And, baby?"

"Yeah?"

"You think they'll give me a side of pickles with my bacon?"

His brows downturned. "Hold up. Your ass wants pancakes, pickles, *and* bacon?"

"And French toast," I added.

Harlan wagged his head. "Our daughter's got some wild ass taste-buds already."

I grinned while lacing his fingers with mine. "Don't kill our vibe, babe. I'm just the messenger."

"Shit, I don't care if it's pickles and pancakes or chocolate and Hot Cheetos. I'll give you both the world," he promised before gently kissing my forehead.

———

The scent of freshly brewed coffee and sizzling bacon enveloped my nostrils and tastebuds as soon as we entered the cozy diner. We settled into a corner booth, and I rubbed my belly while looking over the menu and whispering sweet nothings to our unborn daughter. I peered over the menu to see that Harlan already had his eyes trained on me. His gaze was soft and caring. It was as if all the love he had in his heart for me was on display for the world to see.

The diner hummed around us, a witness to our whirlwind love story, as I stared back at him with a smile. I hadn't expected to fall for a man like Harlan or start a new chapter of my life with him by my side. But I couldn't have been prouder to be his girl and carry his seed. Our love story was unorthodox, but it brought me the most happiness I'd ever experienced. We sat there, hearts and souls entwined from across the table, ready to embark on our journey of love and parenthood together, one breath and one heartbeat at a time.

The End

Afterword

A note from K.L. Hall.

Reader,

Thank you for reading *"Good Girls Always Got A Thing for the Thugs."* If you've made it this far, I hope you'll consider telling me what you thought about the book in the form of a **five-star review and/or rating**. Don't hesitate to let me know what you'd like to see from me next! I thoroughly enjoy reading your thoughts and hearing from you as well! I'm always striving to attract new readers and retain current ones, and reviews are one of the easiest ways to attract readers. If you loved the book, tell a friend, and most importantly, let me know!

All my love,
K.L. Hall

About the Author

K.L. Hall is a national best-selling and award-winning author. As a serial storyteller, Hall has penned over three dozen titles in various genres—including African American urban fiction and romance, paranormal, children's books (as Kimberley M.), and non-fiction. Her fictional stories straddle the intersection of classic Urban and spell-binding Romance.

Highly Acclaimed Titles:

In the Arms of a Savage: (Peaked at #1 in Women's Fiction)

The Potomac Falls Series (Peaked at #1 and #2 in African American Erotica)

Sign up for my mailing list to stay updated with new releases, giveaways, sneak peeks, and more! Click this link: https://bit.ly/38RMpV5

Connect with me on social media:

Facebook: https://www.facebook.com/authorklhall

Twitter: https://twitter.com/authorklhall

Instagram: https://www.instagram.com/officialklhall/

Website: https://www.authorklhall.com

Other novels by K.L. Hall:

Diary of a Hood Princess 1-3

Rise of a Street King: The Justice Silva Story *(Spin-Off to the Diary of a Hood Princess series)*

Broken Condoms and Promises 1-3

In the Arms of a Savage 1-3

Built for a Savage: Blaze and Camille's Love Story *(Spin-Off to the In the Arms of a Savage Series)*

A Ruthle$$ Love Story 1-3

Fallin' for the Alpha of the Streets 1-2

The Most Savage of Them All: The Wolfe Calloway Story *(Prequel to the In the Arms of a Savage Series)*

When a Gangsta Loves a Good Girl

Caught Between My Husband and a Hustler

The Illest Taboo 1-2

To the Only Thug I'll Ever Love

A Lover's Heist: Chief and Gianna's Love Story

A Lover's Heist II: Rome and Lira's Love Story

A Lover's Heist III: Baby and Skai's Love Story

Crushed Velvet & Cashmere

Crushed Velvet & Cashmere 2

Entanglements

Never Had a Bad Boy Love Me So Good

Good Girls Always Got A Thing for the Thugs

Short Reads + Novellas:

Bi-Curious: An Erotic Tale

Bi-Curious 2: Tastes Like Candy

A Savage Calloway Christmas *(Christmas novella to the In the Arms of a Savage Series)*

Lovin' the Alpha of the Streets: A Valentine's Day Novella *(Valentine's Day novella to the Fallin' for the Alpha of the Streets Series)*

Awakened: A Paranormal Romance

As Long as You Stay Down

Solace in Seven

Solace II: The Final Cut

Something Bleu

Something Borrowed

Something New

The Knight Before Christmas: A Potomac Falls Short

I'll Be Home for Christmas: A Potomac Falls Short Book II

Triggered: A Potomac Falls Novella

Wasted Off You: A Friends to Lovers Novella
Because You Don't Know My Name: A Potomac Falls Novella
Will You Say My Name: A Potomac Falls Novella Book Two
Remember My Name: A Potomac Falls Novella Book Three
Every Thug Needs a Lady: A Lady and the Tramp Retelling
Ten Things I Hate About Lovin' You: An Enemies to Lovers Novella
In Exchange: An Urban Thriller

Children's Books:
Princess for Hire
Princess Twinkle Toes & the Missing Magic Sneakers
Little One, Change the World
Adjust Your Crown: A Self-Love Coloring Book for Children of Color

Non-Fiction:
Authors are a Business: The Booked & Busy Course Mini Book

BLP

Visit bit.ly/readBLP to join our mailing list for sneak peeks and release day links!

Let's connect on social media!
Facebook - B. Love Publications
Twitter - @blovepub
Instagram - @blovepublications

We hate errors, but we are human! If the B. Love team leaves any grammatical errors behind, do us a kindness and send them to us directly in an email to blovepublications@gmail.com
with ERRORS as the subject line.

As always, if you enjoyed this book, please leave a review on Amazon/Goodreads, recommend it on social media and/or to a friend, and mark it as READ on your Goodreads profile.

By the Book with B Podcast: bit.ly/bythebookwithb